WITHDRAWN

BOOK III

Lessons from Underground

Master DIPLEXITO and Mr. SCANT

Lessons from Underground

Bryan Methods

CAROLRHODA BOOKS
MINNEAPOLIS

Carolrhoda Books
A division of Lerner Publishing Group, Inc.
241 First Avenue North
Minneapolis, MN 55401 USA

For reading levels and more information, look up this title at www.lernerbooks.com.

Additional image: © iStockphoto.com/Roberto A Sanchez (paper background).

Main body text set in Bembo Std regular 12.5/17.
Typeface provided by Monotype Typography.

Library of Congress Cataloging-in-Publication Data

Names: Methods, Bryan, author.
Title: Lessons from underground / Bryan Methods.
Description: Minneapolis : Carolrhoda Books, [2018] | Series: Master Diplexito and
    Mr. Scant ; [book 3] | Summary: Mr. Scant and his protégé Oliver Diplexito are
    recruited by Scotland Yard to stop Aurelian Binns from stealing a diamond from
    the British Crown Jewels, selling it to a South African en route to America on the
    Titanic, and using the proceeds to fund a criminal secret society in France.
Identifiers: LCCN 2017044212 (print) | LCCN 2017057783 (ebook) |
    ISBN 9781541523746 (eb pdf) | ISBN 9781512405811 (th : alk. paper)
Subjects: | CYAC: Robbers and outlaws—Fiction. | Apprentices—Fiction. |
    Vigilantes—Fiction. | Diamonds—Fiction. | Titanic (Steamship)—Fiction. |
    Cape Town (South Africa)—History—20th century—Fiction. | South Africa—
    History—1909-1961—Fiction.
Classification: LCC PZ7.1.M49 (ebook) | LCC PZ7.1.M49 Le 2018 (print) | DDC
    [Fic]—dc23

LC record available at https://lccn.loc.gov/2017044212

Manufactured in the United States of America
1-39236-21113-4/24/2018

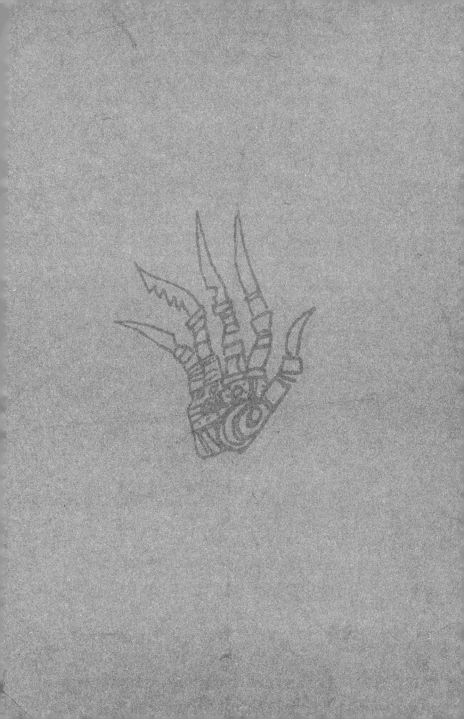

I

The Smugglers' Caves

T he caves were pitch black, but Mr. Scant insisted we use the dimmest light possible. The thieves would have their lamps lit brightly, he said, and he wanted to see them before they saw us. But our smudge of light did next to nothing to show the way, and I was finding it hard to breathe with all that darkness pressing down on me.

We were in the St. Clement's Caves in the sea-side resort town of Hastings. Apparently the caves were pleasant during the summer months, and even attracted royalty for candlelit strolls. But just now it was a cold April night, and the cave was dark, silent, and more than a little creepy. I pressed closer to Mr. Scant, trying not to imagine stepping on an adder or feeling a spider fall down the back of my neck, but he only moved away from me. I had confidence in my mentor, of course, but found myself wondering what I'd do if he rushed off and left me here in the nothingness.

We were in pursuit of a gang of thieves who had broken into the Royal Pavilion in Brighton, two or three hours away by motorcar. They had stolen many of the fine vases and fixtures that the former queen had put on display there. Mr. Jackdaw, our contact at Scotland Yard, said his trusted sources spotted the gang going into what they called the "old smugglers' caves." These sources apparently weren't capable of doing anything about it, though, which is where Mr. Scant and I became useful.

"If we can clear up this little problem without too much kerfuffle, the higher-ups will take my intelligence network more seriously," Mr. Jackdaw had told me on the telephone. "And there's a reward from the mayor of Brighton in it for you, so I'd call that worthwhile. Wouldn't you?"

And so here we were, late at night in the chilly caves. At times like this, Mr. Scant's gift for stealth only made things worse, because I all too easily pictured myself alone but for a ghostly lantern floating beside me. Every time I turned my head, I silently begged the darkness not to spew forth whatever terrifying things it was concealing. The entrance to the caves had made them seem almost civilized, with graceful arches carved into the rock. Now all I could think about were spiders and bats and scorpions and the vengeful ghosts of dead smugglers.

That was a bad frame of mind to be in when Mr. Scant's lantern caught something in the darkness: a hideous face, a vision of the Inferno. I stifled a yell but realized a second later it was just a carving in the soft rock, something some fanciful artist had hewn in years past. Still, I'd let out a sort of hiccup. I could sense Mr. Scant stop dead beside me, and though there was no way to see his face, I knew it was far scarier than the stone one.

I wondered whether to whisper an apology, but before I could make up my mind, I heard the scuff of Mr. Scant's feet and a small clatter from his lantern—and then the little pool of light got smaller and smaller. Mr. Scant had taken off and left me.

I was stuck. If I started to run, I'd make so much noise we'd be given away—I had practiced, but I didn't have Mr. Scant's ability to move silent as an owl. That left me in the middle of the darkness, surrounded by smugglers' ghosts and possibly the thieves themselves. I felt unsteady on my feet, as though my knees were about to give out under me. And then the silence was broken by a gruff and angry voice. "This way!" Mr. Scant called.

I understood at once—Mr. Scant didn't care about giving away our position. There was no more need for silence.

I set off running after him. Part of me was scared of what would happen when we found the miscreants, but my relief from putting the shadows and phantasms out of my head was far greater. The feeling only grew stronger as the light grew brighter—Mr. Scant had adjusted the lamp, allowing me to see the uneven cave floor and the bare rock walls. But as yet I could not tell what had spurred him into action.

Still in his valet's uniform, with the infamous claw ready at his side, he appeared to be running directly for a wall at the end of the rocky cavern, with no sign of stopping. I had already called out, "Wha—?!" when Mr. Scant barged into the wall shoulder-first. It gave way with a terrible cracking sound—not brick at all but some sort of flimsy wood, such as we used for the backdrops of embarrassing plays at school. Mr. Scant must have spotted the wall for a fake.

Through the hole in the false wall, I could see someone swing a long, heavy weapon, a pickaxe or even a sledgehammer. Then the deafening report of a pistol echoed through the cave. But I could also see Mr. Scant jumping this way and that, so the shot must have missed.

Once I burst through the gap, my training took over. I wasn't the scared, useless boy I had once been. Many hard and painful lessons with Mr. Scant had taught me what I ought to be doing in this sort of situation.

Mr. Scant was to my right, low to the ground because he had just kicked the feet out from under one of the thieves. A small revolver lay nearby. Four men in total were holed up in the small hideout, surrounded by golden clocks, chandeliers adorned with dragon statues, and piles of expensive-looking fabric that were most likely curtains. I worked out the greatest threat to me and my ally: the biggest man, who had propped himself up on his elbows after getting knocked flat. He looked ready to grab a spade nearby.

With a fierce yell that came out a bit more high-pitched than I wanted it to, I kicked away the weapon and then did what Mr. Scant's associate Dr. Mikolaitis had taught me to do when fighting a bigger opponent. I jumped on him, punched him in the throat, and then jabbed at his eyes with my fingers. He gave a strangled howl of pain, then made a grab for me. Luckily I didn't have to deal with the consequences of my actions. Mr. Scant pushed me away and rolled the man over, pulling his arms behind his back and tying them together.

Full of energy, I jumped to my feet and shouted, "That's the way to do it!"

Mr. Scant gave me a sharp look, then set about lining up the subdued thieves. One was unconscious, but the others were merely dazed. The biggest man, who had the kind of bald head that connected to his body with no need for a neck, spat out a tooth.

"Try to get everything arranged before we take it out of here," Mr. Scant said.

I looked over at the pile of fabric. "The curtain falls on another ill deed," I said, and grinned. Mr. Scant wasn't amused.

"If there is a time and a place for puns, which I doubt, this emphatically isn't it," he said. "The arrogant man is always the first to fall."

With that, he turned his attention to the gang of thieves. He knelt in front of them, resting his forearm on his knee so that the claw was visible, which is what he did when he wanted to be especially intimidating. As I set about trying to fold the huge embroidered curtains, I listened to his interrogation.

"I'll have you tell me who put you up to this."

"Who says anyone put us up to it?" said the oldest, thinnest man. I could tell just from his voice that he was sneering. He sounded like the kind of person who would spit on the ground a lot—like what was inside him was so unpleasant he tried to get it out all the time.

"You know who I am. You know this claw."

"You're meant to be locked up," said a different man, who sounded more worried.

"They didn't get me," said Mr. Scant. "Now, I've never been a true thief, not like they made me out to be. But I made it my business to study the criminals of note in this part of the world. All the gangs and all the bosses. But I don't know you. That means you're new faces—or you've never done anything worth noticing."

"He's got us there, boss," said the second man.

Mr. Scant went on. "So what makes petty thieves decide to steal fineries that once belonged to kings? Someone put you up to this. Helped you inside, told you what to take, set up the transport for a haul this size."

"Nuh-uh!" came a new voice. "That part was my brother, Ernie. He's got a motor truck for hauling coal."

"Shut up!" the oldest man snapped. But it was too late.

"That part you could manage, then. Who helped you with the rest?" asked Mr. Scant.

There was a prolonged silence. By now, Mr. Scant stood above the men, who were squirming under his fiery gaze. I thought perhaps I would move things along a little.

"Was it by any chance someone who said they were from a secret society? Maybe they said if you stole for them, the society would reward you well? Ah! I can tell from the way you're looking at me I've hit on something." I went to stand by Mr. Scant's side, feeling clever. "They told you that the society had powerful friends and, if you did this, maybe you could be part of it? Just steal some items with old magic in them and you can be one of them?"

Other than the older man, who tried well enough to be inscrutable, the thieves had very honest faces. They had almost been nodding along with me right up until the end, when they simply looked bewildered.

"Don't know nothing about no magic," said the one whose brother did the hauling. "We was just supposed to sell it, that's all."

"Shut up!"

"Why? What's the point in shutting up now?"

"Just keep your mouth shut, will you?"

I turned to Mr. Scant. "Sounds like the Woodhouselee Society, at any rate. Maybe they've given up on the magic, though."

"Good," said Mr. Scant. "Magic is all nonsense. And if the Society is stooping as low as this, we'll have little to worry about in future."

"How are we going to get all of this outside?" I asked him. "It's too heavy for me."

"We don't need to concern ourselves about that. The cavalry's here."

He looked back over his shoulder, and I realized someone had crept into the cave behind us without my noticing. I recognized the pointed chin and wide forehead of Mr. Jackdaw, our Scotland Yard contact, who had frozen himself in an exaggerated tiptoeing pose.

"Confound it," he said, straightening up and tugging at his wispy moustache in irritation. "I was sure I could creep up on you this time."

II

The Pavilion

Mr. Jackdaw had brought what he called his minions to clear out the smugglers' caves while he gave us his undivided attention. After the three of us stepped into the early dawn light, he hurried us into a motorcar and instructed the driver to take us to Brighton.

"You can get an hour or two of shut-eye, and then we'll meet the mayor. He'll be very grateful to you. Of course, I shall present you as agents of the Yard."

"But we're not agents of the Yard," said Mr. Scant.

"True enough, but I can't bally well tell them I solicited the help of an old thief and his employer's son, can I? And if I tell them you're the Ruminating Claw, still at large, they'll be hauling you in on suspicion of stealing the *Mona Lisa*."

"Is that still missing?"

"Still missing."

"Maybe we should try and solve that mystery," I grinned. "You should just make us honorary police-men! We do enough favors for you, after all, and we did an excellent job today if I may say so myself."

"What did I say about arrogance?" rumbled Mr. Scant.

Mr. Jackdaw laughed. "Certainly you did well. If I had any influence over the French police, perhaps I would could volunteer you. You may be onto some-thing, though." He flashed that perfect smile of his that never lit up his eyes. "An honorary policeman. There's an idea."

You never could tell what Mr. Jackdaw was thinking, and that was clearly the way he liked it. We first met him in France, and when our investigations there took us to China, he was there waiting for us. I didn't trust him and never knew what he wanted, but so far only good things had come from doing as he said, and Mr. Scant believed it was good to have allies in the Yard.

Still, it unnerved me that Mr. Jackdaw knew much more about me than I did about him. Jackdaw wasn't his real name; I didn't know what was, nor was I privy to his official job title. He was also adept at getting information out of me without my realizing it. I winced, remembering when I confirmed to him in France that my name is Oliver Diplexito, son of Sandleforth Diplexito, founder and chairman of Diplexito Engineering and Combustibles. Mr. Jackdaw also knew that my father's valet and butler, Mr. Scant, had led a double life as the Ruminating Claw, who was known as an infamous thief. To Jackdaw, it was all an open book: that Mr. Scant had never stolen treasures from museums—only taken them from the real thieves and restored them to their rightful places—and that even now, the organization behind the thefts was probably out for revenge.

I awoke to bright sunshine and Mr. Scant gently shaking my shoulder. The rocking of the motorcar and the comforting smell of the leather seats had sent me to sleep. My mouth was dry from the untold minutes I must have left it hanging open, and I covered it with my hand in embarrassment.

"We have arrived, Master Oliver."

I blinked at Mr. Scant, then looked out of the window on my side of the motorcar. Looking back at me with its extravagant domes and pillars and Arabian-style arches was the Brighton Royal Pavilion. A mess of a building but still a striking sight. More than anything else, it was a reminder that princes and kings could make whatever they liked.

"Have you been to the Pavilion before?" Mr. Jackdaw asked me as I stepped out of the motorcar.

"Outside, yes, but never inside."

"What do you think of the grand old place?"

"Hmm. It's as though someone mixed together a fairytale castle, a wedding cake, and some Christmas tree baubles."

Mr. Jackdaw laughed loudly. "Don't tell that to Algernon," he said.

Algernon, or Mr. Mayor to me and Mr. Scant, apparently owed much of his popularity to his love for the Pavilion and his efforts to make it accessible to the people of Brighton. And so he was in a state of great agitation, waiting for what had been stolen to be returned. When Mr. Jackdaw gave him the good news, the anxiety turned into exuberance, and the mayor's bulldog jowls wobbled as he shook our hands. He had gone so far as to wear his mayoral robe to meet us, a long crimson cloak with fur trim, as well as a big golden medallion. Hung about his neck and shoulders with no less than three thick chains, the medallion had the look of some great golden crab clinging to him.

"Thank goodness, thank goodness," he said, and produced a pocket handkerchief to wipe his brow. "You must allow me to thank you. Please come this way!"

He took us to a banquet room inside the Pavilion, decorated with all the opulence one would expect from a palace designed by a king in love with China. Some fixtures were missing in the corners, and a mantelpiece was conspicuously bare—the thieves' handiwork—but a huge central chandelier remained, far too big for them to have removed.

"Please have some tea. It's Lapsang souchong," said the mayor. "Then there's cucumber sandwiches, and I have some raisin cakes too, if that's not too much at breakfast time!"

He was the sort of man Father would call "ebullient," pronouncing it in the same tone he used for "toenails" or "vomit." I could see why people might have elected the man mayor, but I suspected nobody could spend more than ten minutes with him before they got a headache.

"I really can't thank you enough," he enthused. "Never thought you'd be so young. Are you one of those fellows who looks much younger than he is? I can see that being useful in the Yard. Yes, you must be. Try the cake, the recipe won an award last August, best in the region. I'm so grateful you managed to catch the blighters who broke in here. I almost fainted dead away when I saw what had happened, and no mistaking! I'm just trying to understand the reasons. What made us a target? Any insight?"

"Easily salable items," said Mr. Scant. I could tell from the flatness in his voice he wasn't too keen on the mayor either. "And lackluster security measures."

"Now, now," said Mr. Jackdaw.

"No, no, we deserve that," said the mayor. "You're quite right, sir. Yes, we're going to make bally sure this never happens again. You have my word of honor."

"I'm sure you'll do an excellent job," I said, and the mayor beamed.

"Artwork heists have been on the increase again lately," said Mr. Jackdaw.

"Yes, so I read," said the mayor. "I thought after they locked away that dastardly Ruminating Claw fellow we'd be safe, but it doesn't look that way."

I kept my face carefully still, but it was hard not to laugh at this man calling the Claw dastardly with Mr. Scant only a few seats away from him.

"In fairness, the Pavilion is an unusual target for the criminals in question," Mr. Scant said, and I sensed he was talking more to Mr. Jackdaw than to the mayor. "The pattern up until now has been to select artwork with some connection to magic or alchemy."

"It could be the fine artistry here!" the mayor put in.

"Perhaps it's a sign they're almost out of funds," Mr. Jackdaw said, ignoring the mayor. "Surely a good sign? That is, if the different thefts are connected."

"There are subtler ways to raise money, if the law is no impediment," said Mr. Scant. "I have a feeling this was done to get our attention."

Mr. Jackdaw frowned. "The Yard's attention, or something more . . . specific?"

"That's what I'm asking myself too."

A somewhat awkward silence followed. I decided to break it.

"I think I'll have one of those cucumber sandwiches."

Since I'd had so little sleep the night before, breakfast was more like a late supper. As we ate, the mayor gave a glowing account of his hopes for the Royal Pavilion in future. I felt my eyes grow heavy. Fortunately, the mayor soon clapped his hands and announced it was time for our reward.

"As our way of saying thanks . . ." he began,

standing up with such ceremony that we were clearly obliged to get to our feet as well.

Two tall skinny men in powdered wigs—who had evidently been made to arrive early for work and stuff themselves into ceremonial clothes for this moment—came out with plump velvet cushions. Two hinged boxes sat atop them. After lining us up, the mayor said, "It is my great honor to bestow upon you these tokens of our appreciation. Two medals from the people of Brighton, given in thanks to those who do great things for her."

He pinned Mr. Scant's medal to his jacket first and then gave me the same honor. The medals were large gold discs, decorated with what I assumed was the city's crest.

"They've been in storage for a little while, but it was the best I could do at short notice," the mayor said, and laughed raucously.

With that, we thanked him and took our leave. Other workers, free of powdered wigs, were already moving the recovered items back into the pavilion as we left.

"Did you arrange a car back to Tunbridge Wells for us?" said Mr. Scant.

"Of course!" Mr. Jackdaw replied, pretending to

be offended. "Only the best for the special freelance agents of the Yard, what?"

"Is that what you're calling us now?" Mr. Scant asked, rolling his eyes.

"I just hope I can sleep in the car," I said. "I've got school in the morning. I mean, later on this morning."

"No, you don't," said Mr. Jackdaw.

I looked at him inquisitively, but it was clear he wasn't going to explain the remark until I asked. "Why do you say that?"

"The Yard has arranged for you to have the day off. You need to get your forty winks. There's a special meeting at the Yard tomorrow afternoon, and both of you are invited. So of course we've made your excuses for you."

"You'd better un-make them," I said, the exhaustion of the day so far no doubt showing on my face. "Latin and double mathematics I can skip, but at one o'clock, it's the trials for the fencing team. I don't want to miss it. I really don't."

Mr. Jackdaw's grin didn't falter. "We'll make arrangements for you to attend," he said. "Anything for the hero of the day." With that, he turned to show us to our motorcar.

III
En Garde

Until a few months ago, I wanted nothing more than to be the fly-half on the Judner's School rugby team. However, Mr. Prigg the team coach had made it clear—several times over—that he thought I was too small. He suggested I should be a winger, and my training with Mr. Scant meant I had become fairly good at dodging opponents while I ran. But what I really wanted was a say on the team's larger strategy. I grew frustrated after repeatedly seeing the best play in my mind's eye and then watching the others do something else.

After one particularly upsetting match—during which I had explained clearly but perhaps a little too strongly what everyone was doing wrong—Mr. Prigg told me I might do better in individual sports.

"I just want people to listen to me," I told my best friend Chudley at lunch afterward. "When I'm right, anyway."

"Nobody can be right all the time," said Chudley. "I mean, you think having salmon in your sandwich is better than having ham. That's plain wrong. And maybe the play looked different from where Burton was standing. Maybe he wasn't confident in the kick. Or maybe he just panicked and made the wrong choice. Y'know? Not something to be a rotter about."

"I wasn't being a rotter. I just . . . Ah, maybe I *was*. I only want people to listen to me sometimes. I know that if they try it my way, they'll see I know what I'm talking about. I've been . . . doing some special training."

"Honestly, I miss the times when we just had fun playing," Chudley said. "We didn't have to worry about whether we were good at it or not."

We ate in silence for a little while, and then Chudley made the suggestion that changed my sporting ambitions forever. "You know, my big brother used to be captain of the fencing team. Might be a good mix for you—nobody tells you what to do, and you go one-by-one, but you get to be on a team as well. Our team's pretty strong. Maybe you should go for it."

I had taken an introductory fencing class in my first week of secondary school, when everybody got to try out different sports, but that class had been all about how to step forward and backwards and nothing at all to do with swords, so I had chosen rugby. But Chudley's suggestion made sense, so I asked to make the switch.

At the beginning, I found fencing frustrating, with a lot of rules to learn and the rest of the class far more experienced than I was. But thanks to the lessons I'd been through with Mr. Scant and Dr. Mikolaitis, I picked things up very quickly.

The coach called my progress "prodigious." I soon began to look forward to my time in the fencing salle more than anything else at school. I even convinced Chudley to go along with me.

Five months later, it was time for fencing team trials, which determined who would represent the school in national competitions. Despite my progress, I wasn't a match for the boys who had trained for ten years and showed natural talent. Still, I could best most of the other students who weren't already in the team, so I felt optimistic.

Trying out for the school team meant fencing against the current team members and against the head coach, Mr. Michaelov. Later, they would decide on the new team together. After I was called forward, I stepped into position and saluted my first opponent and the judges. I then noticed Mr. Jackdaw standing by the door. He was alongside Dr. Norman, the deputy headmaster, and was grinning as usual. He gave a little nod as I stared at him in bewilderment, but there was no way I could ask him what was going on, so I pulled down my mask as Mr. Michaelov said, *"En garde."*

I was fencing against Cameron, one of the two team members I was confident I could beat. He was tall, with long arms, but also slow, and he often left his arm vulnerable if he missed his attack. At the next signal from Mr. Michaelov—*"Allez!"*—I rushed forward. Cameron stepped back while thrusting his sword out, which often caught people smaller than him, but I knew it was coming. Parrying the blade and lunging in earnest, I caught him on the shoulder. I had my first hit. The red dye on the blunted tip of my épée sword had left a satisfying dot on his jacket.

By the end of the bout, I barely knew who had scored what. Cameron had caught me by surprise a few times, but I kept in mind something Mr. Scant had taught me—to think not where your opponent was but where they would be next—and it got me the victory. I managed to snatch a victory from Crispin Major next, but I had used so much energy that I couldn't beat Richardson after that. Of course Mr. Michaelov beat me comfortably.

When I took off my mask and saluted the coach after my final encounter, my body felt as though there was a furnace inside it. But someone was clapping. Not Mr. Jackdaw, as I first thought, but Elmsmore, the fencing captain—a broad-chested fifteen-year-old who had to shave every lunchtime or he would have little hairs on his chin by five o'clock.

I was so covered in red dots, especially on my chest, that I looked like a child with chicken pox. Other hopefuls were worse off than me, but I suspected some had fared better. When the last boy had been defeated with a flourish, Elmsmore rounded us up. He told us we had all done well and should continue to work on our basics, and then we were dismissed. After thanking the coach, I went to see Mr. Jackdaw.

"Ah, it's Diplexito's boy," he said, feigning surprise. "You remember me? Your father's friend, Mr. Billingsworth?"

With that, I knew that whatever story he'd given

Dr. Norman, the deputy head, it wasn't the same story I knew. "Hello, Mr. Billingsworth," I said. "I'm surprised to see you here."

"Well, this is what I do," Mr. Jackdaw said with his usual grin. "Inspection of standards, including facilities. I saw you fence, though. You did well."

"I'm still a beginner."

"You must be a fast learner, then."

I shrugged. "I can only do my best."

Mr. Jackdaw looked at Dr. Norman and nodded politely. "I think I've seen all I need to here. Excuse me just for a moment." Before Dr. Norman could say anything, he turned away and guided me with one hand behind my neck to the corridor. Even as we walked, he said, "Master Diplexito, it really is time to go. There are people in London we cannot afford to keep waiting."

"I'll change quickly."

"No time."

"I haven't even showered."

"You never shower after games. You just splash water on your hair."

"For Heaven's sake, how do you know that?"

"An informed guess. It's what I used to do at your age. Now I really must insist."

With that, he seized both my shoulders with an iron grip.

"Ouch, that hurts!" I said.

"Then walk faster," said Mr. Jackdaw. "Your clothes and belongings are all in the vehicle."

Outside the school gates, a black motorcar awaited us. The driver wore a cap and glasses and had a bushy moustache. Very little of his actual face was visible. As soon as I was bundled into the back with Mr. Jackdaw beside me, the driver set the car into motion. On the ledge behind our seats was my fencing bag.

"Where are my clothes?" I asked.

"They're not in your bag?"

"They were hanging on my peg."

Mr. Jackdaw chuckled just a little. "If you want something done properly, do it yourself," he uttered with a dark look toward the driver, who sank down in his chair.

"Our apologies," he said to me. "I'm afraid it would probably be best for you to stay in your fencing clothes."

"But I've got all these marks all over me."

"I'll be sure to explain if anybody asks. It's not such a strange thing to see a boy your age out and about in sports clothes."

"With this many marks, they'll probably think I'm terrible," I said. Mr. Jackdaw showed no sympathy.

We reached our destination after about an hour and a half, but it wasn't where I was expecting. "I thought we were going to Scotland Yard," I said, as the driver brought the motorcar to a halt. Mr. Scant and I had visited Mr. Jackdaw there several times already, in the grand new buildings overlooking the River Thames near Big Ben.

"Quite," said Mr. Jackdaw as he opened his door. "The actual Scotland Yard. You must be thinking of New Scotland Yard."

I didn't know London all that well, but I knew we were in the city center, surrounded by the grand buildings of Whitehall. I could see Trafalgar Square not far away, with the statue of Admiral Horatio Nelson silhouetted against the cloudy sky. "I've never thought how strange it is to have such a big column underneath a statue until just now," I said to Mr. Jackdaw. "Nobody can see Admiral Nelson properly."

"I like it," said Mr. Jackdaw. "You look at it and you know at once how important it is. It does exactly what it's supposed to do, immediately. A fine thing, wouldn't you say?"

Mr. Jackdaw led me away from Whitehall, into a side road and toward a cobbled courtyard. The road signs said it was called Great Scotland Yard. I had wondered before how Scotland Yard got its name, not being located in any such a place, and I supposed I had my answer.

To my surprise, Mr. Jackdaw then led me to a public house named The Rising Sun. When the landlord saw us, he nodded and pulled up a part of the bar for us to pass through. Mr. Jackdaw nodded at him, and I did the same, though the landlord was obviously confused to see me in my breeches. We went down into the cellar, past numerous barrels of beer and bottles on racks. At one of the biggest barrels, Mr. Jackdaw stopped.

"We don't officially use these buildings anymore," he said, producing a key and then twisting aside the tap of the beer barrel to reveal a keyhole. "In fact, there's no way to use the front door. But the rooms here still have their uses."

The barrel was a fake, and after its key was turned, it swung open on hinges, with a whole section of the wall attached. Inside was a tunnel through the earth, which led to a small wooden door. Once through the door, we climbed a flight of stairs back to ground level and found ourselves inside a building much like any other. A lady waiting at a small desk smiled at us as we passed. Up another set of stairs was a door that led into a spacious office.

When I saw who was waiting for us, I couldn't help but smile. Of course, Mr. Scant was there, but two others stood to greet me as well.

"Miss Gaunt! Miss Cai!" I said. Elspeth Gaunt gave a polite nod while Cai Zhao-Ji grinned and got to her feet. After the last time we spoke, I wasn't sure this was a sight I'd see again. But she walked over to me with the help of two walking sticks topped by jade carvings of little birds.

"Wonderful to see you again, Ollie!" she said, taking her walking sticks in one hand and embracing me with the other. "My, you've grown! But what in the world are you dressed up as?"

IV

Interruption

Of the many people in the room, only Miss Cai smiled and shook my hand, but somehow I couldn't help but smile too, as though I had just stepped into a birthday party rather than a blank-walled room with a big square table.

The other attendees were not what you would generally call happy people. Mr. Scant was there with one eyebrow raised. His niece, Miss Gaunt, looked on with her usual reserved expression. Mr. Jackdaw went to take his place at an empty seat at the far side of the room, nodding respectfully at an old man at the head of the table. There were a few other strangers there as well, with faces like chess players.

I mumbled an explanation for why I was in my fencing gear—with no help from Mr. Jackdaw—and took my seat next to Mr. Scant.

"So . . ." I said, clapping my hands together like businessmen always did in plays.

"Let me make introductions," Mr. Jackdaw said. "First, our chair today is Sir Frederickson, my superintendent."

Sir Frederickson was a man with a lot of hair on his chin and none on the top of his head. Heavy wrinkles across his forehead made him look like one of those funny pictures of a face that you can turn upside down to see a different face.

After that, Mr. Jackdaw went around the table, introducing various other police officers, personal secretaries, and other officials with jobs I'd never even heard of. There were also representatives from France, Germany, Austro-Hungary, Russia, Egypt, Canada, and the United States. What was remarkable was how similar they looked—all older men going a little bald but with thick beards and moustaches. Only the American man looked approachable, if a little uninterested.

After Miss Cai had taken her seat again, she and Miss Gaunt were introduced as the "Chinese representative and her associate," and Mr. Scant and I as "the independent agent we mentioned earlier and his apprentice." The strangest part was Mr. Jackdaw's remark that, in present company, he was "Mr.

Richards." I had always known "Jackdaw" wasn't his real name, and I supposed he had a variety of them, but a name as plain as "Richards" didn't suit him at all.

Sir Frederickson, the chair, took charge after the introductions. "Now, we are here to continue discussions commenced February of this, the year of our Lord 1912, regarding the hypothetical foundation of an international police force."

I caught Miss Cai's eye and realized I must have let my feelings show on my face, because she almost laughed. This was a very important meeting, but it didn't sound like it was going to be at all interesting. She leaned over to Miss Gaunt and whispered something to her, whereupon Miss Gaunt also looked over to me. As the French representative began to object to some particular word of what Sir Frederickson had said, Mr. Scant's niece got up, came over to me, and nodded to the door. Nobody paid the slightest attention when an associate and an apprentice slipped out.

"Thank you," I said as we made our way over to a little window. It had metal bars, as if we were in a cartoon prison, though presumably to stop anybody from breaking *in* rather than out. "I'd rather talk with you than sit in there in silence. It's good to see you!"

"It's good to see you too," said Miss Gaunt,

though as usual it was hard to tell if she meant it or if she was being polite. "Zhao-Ji said you would be bored, so I should keep you entertained."

"Well, you don't have to if you don't want to . . ."

"Ah, I should have said first that I'd rather talk with you as well. I've already read the agenda for the meeting and I know what they're all going to say. Nothing will be decided today, but we will be a little closer than before."

"You and Miss Cai are still trying to form the international police force, then? I suppose it's not easy to convince a crowd like that. They wouldn't listen to me, of course. I'm not old or beardy enough."

"Perhaps the problem is that Zhao-Ji isn't either." I expected a smile from Miss Gaunt as she said this, but she looked back to the door wistfully. "If they only listened to her, this would all have been decided months ago."

"I'm not sure we should be here," I said. "Mr. Jackdaw said it was a kind of reward for us for helping him, but I think they want to pretend Mr. Scant works for them."

Miss Gaunt gave a thoughtful little nod. "They all know who my uncle is by now. It may not seem like it to you, but the operation in China last summer was an excellent example of nations sharing information and working together. And Zhao-Ji and I have argued it would be an even better example had we shared more from the beginning. The idea that we all had to rely on a civilian as much as we did, one who may or may not have a criminal past, is embarrassing for proud men. And women, for that matter."

"It sounds as though you don't like these people very much."

"Does it? Oh dear, I'm not good at hiding my feelings."

I tried not to laugh. "That's kind of sweet, in a way."

Miss Gaunt shot me an irritated look, and for a moment unnervingly resembled her uncle. "I don't want to be sweet."

"Sorry."

She gave a little shrug, then looked over the numerous red marks on my fencing jacket. "Have you spoken to my father about fencing? He was very keen on it when I was a child."

"Really? Uncle Reggie? I had no idea."

"I ought to write him a letter. How is he?"

"He's doing well. He and Aunt Winnie just got a new cat. They've called it Baroness von Cuddlepaws.

I hope they never have to say that name in public . . . Is something wrong?"

For a brief moment, I thought I might have seen a pained expression on Miss Gaunt's face.

"Nothing at all," she said, producing a paper fan from her sleeve and flicking it open to fan herself—which only made her seem more agitated. "Although . . ." She sighed to herself. "You call Father and Mother by their names, but you continue to call me 'Miss Gaunt.' Are we still strangers?"

At first I didn't know what to say. "Of course we're not strangers. I didn't realize you felt that way. Certainly I can call you Elspeth. Or Ellie, if you prefer."

Her usual blank expression was back in place when she nodded and said, "Ellie will do just fine."

"Ellie it is," I said. "And of course, you must call me Ollie. Ha, Ellie and Ollie. What a pair, huh?"

No response came from her this time. She was staring intently at something out of the window.

"We need to move," she said, putting her hand on my shoulder.

"What did you see?" I asked, but she just urged me toward the meeting room. As I stumbled, I heard the sound of cracking wood from downstairs and the voice of the woman at the reception crying out before going silent. Several men, including Mr. Scant, rose to their feet the moment they saw us burst through the meeting room door.

"Intruders!" I yelled.

Miss Cai was already pushing herself to her feet. "How many?"

"Unconfirmed," Ellie said. "At least four, but I think many more."

"Dammit, Frederickson, what is this?" yelled the American man. The younger men, most of them bodyguards or Scotland Yard agents, reached for weapons, but then three of them turned pistols on their opposite numbers across the table. There was a lot of shouting and swearing in different tongues. Mr. Jackdaw attempted to dash for a side door, but someone in black pushed his way through it and pointed a revolver at him. At the same moment, the intruders from downstairs reached the main door, and Ellie pushed me back protectively. A number of men surged in, all in black three-piece suits and all armed. One made note of us in the corner and took up a position where he could keep an eye on us.

"Let's be calm and see what they want," Sir Frederickson said, a snarl on his lips. He was looking askance at one of the young men from Scotland Yard.

The young agent must have turned traitor, because he was aiming at his superior with one of two pistols. He pointed the other at an Austro-Hungarian bodyguard with a revolver of his own.

"Sensible as always, Sir Frederickson," came the voice of a young man who swept in behind the others, removing his top hat. He was dressed in finer clothes than the others, almost like a dandy—a navy blue Inverness greatcoat, with his black hair worn long and swept back fashionably. He was a young man, only seventeen or eighteen, clean-shaven with a lean, handsome face and heavy brows. I recognized him instantly, even though I had only seen him once before, on the streets of Paris.

"Good day to you all," he said smoothly. One of his men brought him a chair so that he could sit at the table.

I wasn't the only one to realize who he was. In the chaos, Mr. Scant had somehow managed to put on his claw, and he made no move to conceal it. But rather than rushing at one of the intruders, he lowered himself back into his chair. "If it isn't young Master Binns," he said.

Aurelian Binns grinned like a wolf. "The very same."

V

Diamonds and Photographs

Sir Frederickson's eyes widened as Aurelian Binns leaned back in his chair and put his boots up on the table. Two men stood close behind him with black coshes while others continued to hold their guns ready.

"What a pleasure, to finally be amongst such esteemed company," Aurelian said, running a hand back through his hair. "It was a shock not to receive an invitation."

"Who is this?" demanded Sir Frederickson. "This is an outrage."

"You remember the debriefing on the Woodhouselee Society affair, sir?" Mr. Jackdaw answered. "This is Roland Binns's son, Aurelian."

"How did you get in here?" Sir Frederickson snapped.

"I asked nicely. But of course, *how* is such a small-minded question. Rather, you should want to know *why*. Hello, Mr. Scant. Master Diplexito. What a peculiar thing to wear."

Mr. Scant stayed silent, so I did the same, while Ellie stepped in front of me. There was contempt under Aurelian's smile, but also the confidence of one who felt completely protected.

"So tell us why you're here and what you want," the Egyptian representative said.

"Just one moment, Mr. Bashi, if you please," Aurelian said. "One of us here has an inclination toward sudden and rather mindless violence. Mr. Scant, please have a look at this photograph. Careful now—it's a little old."

He took his feet down from the table and slid a small photograph over to Mr. Scant. I couldn't make it out well from where I stood with Ellie, but I thought I could see a building in the picture. Mr. Scant took a deep breath as he looked upon it, his expression darkening.

"I know you won't need me to explain," Binns said. "And now, ladies and gentlemen—to business. I want to make it clear, very clear, that this little project you're putting together, this, ah, endeavor—it will not happen. An international police force, all nations cooperating. No, no, it will never work. I'm against it. Policing a state is one thing, but the world? That's called authoritarianism. A long word, I know, but those of us with only an American education can look it up later."

The American representative bristled but said nothing.

"Besides, suppose you all manage to put your differences aside, forget all about who killed who in the last war and whose spies will be the first to exploit this new arrangement. Even then, I'm afraid there's another conflict of interest when it comes to international police. That would be between you and me—and my many partners and associates. If you start chattering to one another about this criminal here and his links to that group there, why, that would make things much harder for me. So I've made it my business to ask you—nicely—to stop. Half of you will probably be at war with the other half by the time you get the idea up and running, in any case."

"How does a boy like you think he will stop us?" growled the Frenchman.

"Disruption, *m'sieur*," Aurelian said, his white

teeth flashing again. "I don't deny your combined resources would outstrip almost any force in the world. And if my men and I decide to attack your organizations, no doubt we will be beaten, foiled, even locked away. But each time, you'll encounter more disruption—and with that, more repairs, more to pay. It will cost you too much to keep trying and trying."

"Criminals can't stop the progress of justice," said Miss Cai. "The world is ready for international cooperation, and there's too much for us to gain for you to stop us forever."

"I don't need to stop you forever, though I rather hope I do," Aurelian said, looking at his nails. "But in hundreds of years, you've never been able to achieve international cooperation, much less maintain it. Do you know who *has* perfected it? Those of us who work from the shadows. Secret societies the world over are connected in ways you'll never understand."

"Criminals, you mean," said Ellie.

"Criminals indeed, for what is a criminal but one who rejects control, the rule of law? We can run rings around any joint police force you cobble together, and we will. But nobody wants to make more effort than we have to, so can we all agree that the idea's unnecessary? Leave the whole unpleasant business behind us?"

"Run rings around us?" repeated the American. He laughed raucously. "This little dude comes in here, making big claims, and he hasn't even started shaving yet. Why are we taking him seriously?"

"What's a dude?" I whispered to Ellie.

"I can understand why you would have doubts," Aurelian said. "So here's what I'll do. I'm going to follow one of the feats of the Ruminating Claw—I'm sure you've heard of him. As all the world knows, that man was my father." He gave a chuckle with no humor in it and looked directly at Mr. Scant's claw, still resting on the table.

"Yes, the famous Claw, we all read, not only plucked the Sword of Mercy from amongst the Crown Jewels in the Tower of London, but put it back again a day later without anyone catching him. What a feat." His eyes narrowed. "Sons do like to outdo the feats of their fathers. So I shall do one better. I'm going to take the King's Sceptre with Cross. You know the one. Not so long ago, our beloved king had the largest diamond in the world added to it.

"I have a buyer, you see, who I've arranged to meet on a very expensive voyage bound for America. He's going to take the diamond back to Africa—I'm helping to return it home! How kind of me. And the funds I accrue will make quite the difference for my new society over in France. Ah, it will be a glorious thing, the birth of a *true* international power. Rising again, like the proverbial third day. That's a good name, isn't it? The Third Day Society." He paused for effect, but nobody said a word, so he continued.

"Let it be a test, then. A theft in London, a buyer from the Union of South Africa, a voyage bound for America, the proceeds going to France. Your country, your country, yours, and—well, a colony under your jurisdiction. A suitably international stage, wouldn't you say?"

The American was not impressed. "You don't scare me. You don't scare any one of us around here. Why don't we just shoot you now?"

"Well, Mr. Carr, you could. But I think you're all going to want to exit this meeting room very quickly."

It was then that Ellie's hands squeezed tighter on my shoulders. I looked back and saw her sniffing the air. That's when I smelt it too, and stared in alarm at the rivulets of black smoke creeping in under the door.

"Ha, you've noticed," Aurelian said with a smile. "Perfect timing. Don't anybody move. My men and I are the guests here, so I hope you will be polite enough to let us depart first."

"Noticed what exactly?" said Sir Frederickson.

"Burning," I said. "I think the building's on fire."

VI
A Picture from the Past

"**N**one of you move an inch," Aurelian said, deadly serious for the first time. He lifted one finger, at which his men tensed, ready to fire their pistols. Nobody moved.

"We'll be going ahead of you," said Aurelian. "Now, you may already be thinking about what to do when we begin to exit. How to pursue us, the best moment to catch us, how to signal that these bodyguards should protect your man while you give chase. So that's why this is necessary."

For a moment, I saw Mr. Scant pushing himself away from the table—then I flinched at the deafening sound of pistols. Someone was screaming in pain, a deep, guttural, desperate sound. But all I could see was the men in suits filing out. Then Aurelian himself was before me in the corner, pausing to smirk. He looked at me with the same hatred I remembered on his father's face. Then he was gone.

"Should we go after him?" Ellie said, helping Miss Cai to her feet. I tried to assist them, but Miss Cai only asked if I was all right. When I nodded, she turned to Ellie.

"We need to get out of here. And take the injured with us."

"Injured?" I said, looking over to the table. A few of the old men were groaning and clutching at their thighs—shot in the legs, to slow us down. Mr. Scant had taken one of Sir Frederickson's arms on his shoulder, helping him to stand.

"Mr. Scant, what should I do?" I asked.

"Make sure the route is clear," said Mr. Scant. "We've got four injured. They tried to get me too, but I was ready for it. Go."

Miss Cai urged Ellie to go with me. Ellie insisted she'd be back to help as soon as the way was clear, and then we set off after Aurelian and his men. There was no sign of them, save for the rapidly thickening smoke.

"What do we do if we catch up to Aurelian?" I said.

"It's unlikely," said Ellie, no trace of fear in her

voice. "If we do, we cannot fight them all. So we stay back until we can make sure the others have a way out."

We rushed down the stairs and found the secretary lying back in her chair, unconscious. In the corners of the hall, the fire was spreading to the bookshelves and the old clock. Aurelian's men had dropped oily rags behind them to help feed the flames.

"We have to help her," I said.

"The route first," Ellie said.

I nodded, but I stopped after just one step. "We can't just leave her with the fire."

Ellie looked back at me as though I had been speaking another language. She sighed and said, "I'll get her ready. You check our route. I'll see if there's a way through the old main doorway, though since we all had to come through that tunnel, I assume it's been permanently blocked."

"All right," I said, and hurried down the steps into the basement passage. Nothing was aflame down there, but the heat was unbearable. I ran until I reached the public house next door, and when I hurried up the steps, I saw a terrible scene. The place was wrecked, glass bottles smashed everywhere, tables and chairs strewn over the floor and nobody in sight.

With all that spilled alcohol, the place would be an inferno soon enough.

I checked the pub's window to make sure Aurelian's men weren't waiting for us in the courtyard outside, then tried the door. Locked. I knew that in my current state of mind, I'd take too much time to pick the lock. I would have to break the big window.

I grabbed an unbroken bottle of gin that lay on the floor and threw it with all my strength—but the window didn't break. Stepping closer to see if I'd at least cracked the glass, I met someone's eye and ducked out of sight. But there was no need to hide. It was a fearsome face but a welcome one—the scarred, fiercely intelligent face of Dr. Mikolaitis, Mr. Scant's oldest ally.

He gestured for me to stand back. A moment later, a brick smashed through the glass. Then the doctor was up on the sill, his gloved hands pushing out the remaining shards.

"What happened?" he said.

"We were attacked," I said, "by Aurelian Binns."

"Not exactly a surprise," he said. "Where's Scant?"

"Helping the others. We have to help them too."

"You wait outside."

"No. I can still help. Maybe more than you can."

Dr. Mikolaitis gave me a stern look, his hand going to the shoulder where he had been shot the year before. But he nodded.

"This way," I said, and led him back to the secret meeting house. The fire was completely out of control, and there were shouts and cries from the men trying to get the injured down the stairs as we arrived. Ellie was struggling with the receptionist, while Miss Cai stood at the top of the stairs with her walking sticks, shouting instructions.

"Dr. Mikolaitis, help her!" I said. The doctor was a strong man, but he grunted in pain as he knelt to pick the woman up and put her over his shoulder.

"Are you okay? Your wound . . ."

"It's . . ." Dr. Mikolaitis began, but he didn't finish. "Just help me stand."

Ellie I helped support the receptionist's weight as the doctor got to his feet. A little unsteadily, he made for the stairs.

I hurried to Mr. Scant and told him the way was clear. He nodded, bounded up the steps, and grabbed Miss Cai's walking sticks, tossing them to me to catch.

"As we agreed," Miss Cai said to Mr. Scant.

"I will not be carried like a sack of potatoes."

Mr. Scant nodded, kneeling down so that she could climb onto his back.

I went ahead with Miss Cai's sticks, helping everyone get the injured safely down the basement steps and back up into the public house. The fire was even worse when we reached the pub, with most of the floor ablaze, but Ellie pulled down a curtain and used it to dampen the flames long enough us to cross. A bottle at the bar exploded when we passed, but there was no time to stop. We all made a dash for the broken window, using the bench and table beneath it as steps before jumping out to freedom.

As I handed Miss Cai her walking sticks, Ellie pointed to me and said, "You're bleeding."

"I am?" I raised a hand, and Ellie guided it gently to the left side of my neck. I winced.

"Let me," she said. A sudden sharp pain followed, like a bee sting, and then Ellie held up a small shard of glass. I reached instinctively for my pocket hand-kerchief, but of course I was still in my fencing garb, so I didn't have one. Mr. Scant gave me his instead, and I pressed it to the wound. The cut ached, dully, but it was nothing beside the wounds some of the men had suffered.

"You see what they did?" said Miss Cai. "Their targets were all from your British Empire. Britain, Canada, Egypt—British sovereignty. If anybody dies, this could be made to look like a foreign nation attacking Britain."

"Nobody's going to die," Mr. Scant said, moving to help Dr. Mikolaitis wrap a cloth tight around the Egyptian representative's leg. Mr. Jackdaw stumbled toward me, looking crestfallen.

"Made a real fool of me." He was holding the side of his thigh, where the fabric around his improvised bandage was all wet.

"Are you okay?" I asked.

"Cut through the flesh on the side of my leg. A trifling matter compared with the chaps who got hit dead on. I wish I knew how that scoundrel found out about this meeting."

"Don't underestimate the Society," said Dr. Mikolaitis.

"And what are *you* doing here, Doctor?" Mr. Jackdaw said.

"I know how they think, that's all. I was worried."

"Dr. Mikolaitis isn't a traitor," I said. "He hates the Society."

"I know," Mr. Jackdaw said. "But I'm the one

who will have to put all this in a report. From hospital, it would seem. Damn it all."

This was the first time I had seen Mr. Jackdaw look genuinely upset. He'd been so careful with his emotions until now.

It took a long time to bring order to the situation, calling the fire service, the ambulances, the embassies and more. There was a lot of fretting over protocol as the representatives took their leave, and a lot of anger too. Mr. Jackdaw grimly joked that he was lucky he got shot or his supervisors would have been a lot angrier with him. Miss Cai and Ellie excused themselves but said they would be in touch.

"Sorry we dragged you into this," Miss Cai said.

Eventually we took our leave as well, and Dr. Mikolaitis led us to his coach on the Thames Embankment. Although he took the coach to my house every time he tutored me, I hadn't ridden in it since the time Mr. Scant and I had broken its roof by jumping onto it from the top of the National Portrait Gallery. Dr. Mikolaitis took up the driver's seat, behind two fine-looking chestnut horses, while I stepped into the carriage with Mr. Scant. Soon we were in motion, one of the few horse-drawn carriages on Whitehall amongst the motorcars.

"What a disaster," I said. "I'd been worrying about Aurelian. I suppose I was right to worry."

Mr. Scant ignored me. Instead, he drew something out of his jacket pocket. The photograph Aurelian had given him. The picture's subject looked to be a large white building, or at least a color that looked white in a photograph. A simple, unornamented structure with a tree outside that didn't resemble any in England. A small figure stood outside it, too small for me to be able to make out any detail.

"What's in the photograph?" I said in a soft voice.

Mr. Scant gave no reply, just went on staring at the picture as the horses slowly closed the distance between us and home.

VII
Out of Sorts

Back home, Mr. Scant began to behave very strangely. He seemed preoccupied the next day, both in his valet duties and during our training session after school. He barely watched my knife-throwing practice and had no advice to give me. Then he asked me to study the Bow Street Runners even though I'd already written him a report on them.

"Shouldn't I study about Africa?" I asked.

"Why do you say that?"

"Isn't that where Aurelian said the diamond came from? And that there's a 'buyer from the Union of South Africa.' I don't know where that is. I don't know *anything* about Africa, except for ancient Egypt."

"I see, I see," rumbled Mr. Scant. "I don't think I would be much help to you in that regard."

I frowned. This was the first time I'd ever seen Mr. Scant look as though he hadn't already thought of everything I was going to say. "Are you all right, Mr. Scant? What was in that photograph Aurelian showed you?"

"I have no wish to speak of it," Mr. Scant said, and turned away.

That evening, Dr. Mikolaitis came to see Mr. Scant, meeting him in the Ice House—the underground ice store that Mr. Scant had uncovered near my home and made into his lair. When Dr. Mikolaitis emerged, he appeared frustrated.

"Acting strange, isn't he?" I said to him, as I walked with him toward his little coach.

"Yes. Very distracted. It's something to do with his past. That much I learned."

"Aurelian showed him a photograph," I said. "It was of a building, I think—someone in front of it too—but Mr. Scant wouldn't talk about it."

"'Aurelian,' you say?" Dr. Mikolaitis almost laughed. "Why do you still call Heck 'Mr. Scant' and me 'Dr. Mikolaitis,' while the Binns boy is 'Aurelian'?"

"I hadn't really thought about it," I said. "He's too old for me to call him 'Master Binns,' and 'Mr.

Binns' is his father. Maybe I got mixed up because Elspeth Gaunt asked me to call her Ellie. And of course I can't call you or Mr. Scant by your given names. That would be too strange."

"Too strange, is it?" said Dr. Mikolaitis, with a look that made it clear he thought I was the strange one. "Tell me about this photograph. An old one?"

"It looked old. Maybe from another land."

"Africa?" he said.

"Er, maybe. What made you think so?"

"Heck lived there in his youth. Spent time in the Cape Colony, which recently became part of the Union of South Africa. One of the only things I know about his past. That's where he got the scars on his hands."

"Ah! I remember the girls talking about the scars once. Our maids Meg and Penny, I mean. But Mr. Scant told me he didn't know anything about Africa."

Dr. Mikolaitis looked thoughtful. "Is that what he actually said?"

"Well, I don't think those were his words, exactly. He just said he couldn't help me."

"That doesn't mean he doesn't know. Only that he will not speak of it."

We had reached Dr. Mikolaitis's old coach, where

he put the bit back into his horse's mouth and then climbed up into the driver's seat. It was a strange arrangement, a man driving his own coach about and leaving it wherever he chose to step down. But Dr. Mikolaitis was rather a strange man. "You will be needing a lift?" he asked.

"Me? Where to?"

"I thought you wanted to learn of Mr. Scant's past. If he is not willing tell you, and I cannot help you, there's only one man who's known him longer than I have."

"Uncle Reggie," I said. "Yes, please. I'd like to visit him."

Dr. Mikolaitis didn't join me as I called on Mr. Scant's brother. Rather, he left me at Uncle Reggie's doorstep and told me to fetch him from the nearby pub when I was finished. Reginald Gaunt and his wife, Winifred, had moved to a townhouse in Tunbridge Wells to be closer to Mr. Scant, though their new home was a characteristically eccentric one. In the small front garden, two of those ugly garden gnomes from Germany watched me pass from beneath their bright red caps. Somehow, their blank eyes and broad grins reminded me of Mr. Jackdaw. I wondered how he was doing.

I rang the doorbell, and the door was opened by the man Uncle Reggie had hired as his manservant, Mr. Twiggs. He was an elderly fellow, at least seventy, and a little slow but very friendly and good at his job. Though without Mrs. Twiggs, who did the cooking, he tended to forget what he was meant to be doing.

"Who is it?" I heard Uncle Reggie call.

"Come in, come in," said Mr. Twiggs, so I wiped my shoes and stepped inside. Uncle Reggie didn't care for indoor shoes, so everyone walked around his house in socks. Mr. Twiggs led me to the living room, announced me as "the young master," and left it at that.

"Ollie!" said Reginald. "What a delight! Oh, let me get you a slice of cake. We had cake today. You like cake, don't you? What am I saying, everyone likes cake. I'll get you cake."

"You just sit down," came a voice from another room. "We'll bring cake in with the tea."

"Hello, Uncle Reggie," I said, then called to the other room, "Hello, Aunt Winnie! It's me!"

"I saw you from the window, dear!" came the reply. "Be out in a tick!"

"Here, let me get those." As usual, the Gaunts' house was a mess of newspapers, books, an empty ink pot, and what looked like some sort of navigational compass on the sofa. Uncle Reggie gathered all of it up and carried it to a side table, shoving a lamp aside so that he could put it all down.

"How are your injuries?" Poor Uncle Reggie had suffered a terrible beating the year before at the hands of Aurelian Binns's men. He now had a purple bruise across his hairline that didn't seem to fade, though otherwise he seemed to have recovered well.

"I'm not as bad as I might be," he replied. "So what can I do for you today? Has Heck done something dreadful again?"

"Well, it's about him, but he hasn't really done anything. Before that, I should probably tell you we had a run-in with Aurelian. You know, Mr. Binns's son."

"No!" Uncle Reggie's eyes widened as he sat in his comfy chair. "What's the little pustule done this time?"

"He came to stop a meeting about an international police force. Whoops. I'm not sure I'm supposed to tell you that. Anyhow, some people got shot. In their legs, but still. It was a horrible thing."

"You were there during this?"

"Yes."

"Well, are you both all right?"

"They shot at Mr. Scant, but he got out of the way."

"Seems to happen to him a lot."

"Ellie was there too. She's fine. She was looking out for me the whole time."

Uncle Reggie sighed. "Well, that's a good thing, to be sure. Could be worse. Not a bad thing, overall. I do wish I'd hear this news from her, not from you. A father worries about his child. In my day it was unthinkable to go about like that unchaperoned. And right when I thought we could *stop* worrying about her, another Binns . . . I tell you, if I could ask God to shuffle one lineage right off of this mortal coil . . . Ah."

Aunt Winnie and Mrs. Twiggs had appeared. Aunt Winnie brought in all the cups and saucers, plus a plate of snacks, while tiny Mrs. Twiggs held a small tray with the teapot on it. Uncle Reggie lowered his voice and gave a little nod toward his wife. "Best keep mum about this, don't want her worrying overmuch."

"Okay," I whispered. Aunt Winnie didn't notice, as she was keeping a close eye on Mrs. Twiggs and encouraging her with some kind words. It was as though Mrs. Twiggs was the one receiving assistance rather than the other way around, but there was something very sweet about the scene. At their feet, looking up hopefully at the cake, were the two cats—plump, haughty Lady Hortensia and a sleek gray creature who must have been Baroness von Cuddlepaws.

"There now," Aunt Winnie said as she set the trays down and took the teapot from Mrs. Twiggs, who bowed a little and shuffled away. "Nice to see you, Oliver."

"Nice to see you too."

"How are your mother and father?"

"They're doing well, thank you." I would have answered the same if they were lost at sea—it was just the sort of thing you said to be polite.

"That's nice. Oh, Reginald, you could have tidied up a bit more. I keep telling him the place is a pigsty, but he won't listen to me."

I smiled and said nothing. I didn't know Aunt Winnie nearly so well as I knew Uncle Reggie, and although I'd visited many times during Uncle

Reggie's recuperation, I always remembered my first encounter with Aunt Winnie. She had spent most of the time shrieking at me, Uncle Reggie, and Mr. Scant as we tried to escape from Mr. Binns and his men. Now, of course, we pretended none of that had never happened.

"The lad was just telling me about some problem Heck's been having."

"Is that so?" Aunt Winnie said, pulling the little table closer so she could pour the tea.

"Not exactly a problem," I said. "He's just been acting strangely since Aure—I mean, since he saw this old photograph. I think it's from Africa, but he won't tell me anything about it. I don't think he's told anybody about that time. But I'm a little worried, and you've known him longer than anyone else, Uncle Reggie, so I thought you'd be able to tell me something."

Uncle Reggie looked at me contemplatively for a moment, then sat back with a heavy breath, crossing his arms. "Africa, hmm? Now that was a long time ago."

"Were you there too?"

"No. I would have liked to have gone, but Heck went alone. For research."

"He wasn't fighting there?"

"Fighting? Oh! You mean with the Boers? No, no, it was before that business. This happened back when we were only a few years older than you are now. My dear brother was maybe 19 or 20 when he went. Heck trained with the Royal Navy afterwards, yes, but he'd left for university before the first Boer war began. That would have been in . . . the very end of 1880, it started."

"I don't really know about Africa," I said. "Just what I read about Mr. Churchill going to war."

Uncle Reggie seemed to find that very funny. Even Aunt Winnie smiled a little as she handed me a slice of sponge cake with a cherry on the top. "Heck's not a madman like that Churchill."

"Now, now," said Aunt Winnie.

Uncle Reggie leaned forward. "Your Aunt Winifred used to be quite a fan of Mr. Churchill. Thought he was most dashing, didn't you?"

"He's a very brave man," said Aunt Winnie. "I'll thank you not to tease me. He was rather handsome before he went bald."

"He only cares about himself and people who are just like him," Uncle Reggie said. "And it's not that he's brave. He's just addicted to war."

"Then he'll do well as First Lord of the Admiralty, won't he?" Aunt Winnie said, taking a sip of her tea with a haughtiness that matched Lady Hortensia's. "No need to be jealous of his accomplishments."

"Hmmph." Uncle Reggie began loading his tea with his usual copious amount of sugar. "To return to the point, when Heck left England, it wasn't to fight, and there wasn't a war on. Back then, we were dreaming of being scientists. His field and mine were different, of course. England was a good place for chemists, so I was right at home here. Oh, it was a good time, I can tell you. It's grand, being young. Can't recommend growing up in the slightest. But if you want to know why Heck went all the way to the south of Africa, I'd better start at the beginning. Do you need more cake? Well, you're welcome to more if you want it. Now, where shall I begin?"

VIII
Uncle Reggie's Story

"Once Heck and I decided to become scientists, our poor dear mother, who I wish I could go back and thank properly, did all she could to find us chances to study. Some of Father's old navy friends were very helpful too. My field was chemistry, and there was plenty of research for me to do here in England. I did apprenticeships with various Royal Society members. I tell you, if I could relive those times, I would be a happy man! A happy man indeed.

Heck's subject was optics. He was studying to become an engineer, but it was light that fascinated him most. The ways we can bend it and refract it. Luminescence and phosphorescence. You know. Bit of a mystery to me, I have to admit. And you see, back then, and it must have been 1871, or 1872 at a stretch, they had just started digging up those diamonds they're so famous for over in the Cape Colony. Part of the Union of South Africa, as they call it now. Not the big business it is today, when Heck set sail. Just the first rumors of unbelievable riches.

I remember it well. We were sat down for dinner. Our mother, may she forgive me my sins, had made one of her wonderful roast beef dinners, and Heck just sits down and bold as you like, says, 'I'm going to abroad to study diamonds.'

'Study them in your pocket, you mean.' That's what I said, and then we got in trouble because Heck threw a roasted parsnip at me.

In fact, Heck didn't care about the riches—and it's not as though a man there could pick a diamond up in the mud. As soon as the first ones were found, hundreds of people tried getting their hands on them, buying property rights here and claiming family rights there. They called the place New Rush because so many people went, trying to get rich. And some did find their fortunes. But that's not what Heck wanted, and besides, he was much too late for that. His big idea was, well, with so many diamonds being found, he could ask to research some of them, find out what they would do paired with photographic film or lenses or, I don't know, Hertzian waves.

Mother let him go with her blessings, of course. The only thing she asked was who was going to pay for his passage and living costs.

'Captain Pritchard's helping me get sponsored by the Royal Naval Academy,' said Heck. 'He says it's a done deal. I have to enlist in the navy afterwards and get through basic training, but I don't have to do any more than that if I don't want to.'

All our dear old mother had to say after that was, 'Stay safe, you hear?'

We saw him off at the dockside. Portsmouth or Southampton, I don't remember now. Mother was all smiles while she waved her kerchief to him, but had a good cry when she got home—which was bad because it always sets me off too, you know? I'm sure you do.

Anyway, Heck was off. His first adventure out into the world. Can't say I was jealous at the time. I thought he was mad. I suppose I had a very strange idea of Africa at the time—it was all cannibal stories then, all that superstitious nonsense in books. Now I know that if anyone were going to eat him, it would probably be a Dutchman.

You'll have to forgive me if I forget some of the details. This isn't something I've thought about for many a year. Heck's ship would have reached the Cape of Good Hope first, with a trip by land to New Rush after that. It wasn't hard. So many eager young men from all around the world were going there to get rich. Heck would have taken the coach with the rest. I'm sure everyone thought he was just like the others, about to get chewed up and spat out by the bigger fish in the pond. Fish growing into sharks.

The history of the Cape Colony is, well, it's a bit of a tangle. The Dutch were the first from Europe to claim it as their land, landing their ships there and finding the local people, farmers and hunters. The Cape was a useful place to have a port for Dutch trade routes to Asia, so they made a colony.

Over the next hundred, hundred and fifty years, the colony became a big place, with the locals pushed out. But then the Netherlands got taken over by Napoleon, so the Cape became a territory of the French, because the French ruled over the Dutch, you see? Now, that gave Napoleon a base to attack other British colonies and British trade routes to places like India, which of course would not do. So we British go over with our armies and navies and have a battle like we always do. Always seems to be the way.

Well, we win the fight and take over. Obviously, the Dutchmen there weren't exactly happy. They didn't like suddenly being told they weren't Dutch or even French but British. They had been using slaves to expand the colony, slaves bought from traders in the west of Africa. Well, the Dutch definitely didn't like being told they had to free them all, which was the British law. So those Dutchmen went and founded their own little state, which would probably have kept the fighting to a minimum for a moment. Except, of course, with the Lord's usual sense of humor, diamonds had to be found right on the border between these places.

So this is the kind of place Heck came to, if you can imagine it. The other end of the world, in the midst of a rush for riches, where Englishmen were clashing against everyone else who'd come there to get rich, as well as the Dutchmen and the local people too—along with the people who were a mix of both, from when the Dutch and the local people had married each other. Heck had money but he knew nobody. No arrangements for where to stay. All the lodgings were full, of course, even the most dreadful hovels built for the poor mine workers.

But after a while of knocking on doors and finding no rooms, he met a girl who had opened a school for the children of the town. It may not sound like that new township was a place for children, but wherever there are people, there will be children sooner or later. As I recall, this young lady was named Miss Handle—part Dutch, if I recall Heck correctly, but with grandparents from one of the Bantu tribes. A common thing in that part of the world, though it usually means a hard life. But she wanted to start a school and had the means to do it, so I suppose her view was, 'Just you try to stop me . . .'

The way Heck tells it, he was all but collapsing on the floor outside her new school, and she came running out with a glass of water. He thought she was awfully kind, until she asked him if he was really a man, fainting like that just from being in the sun. Well, I suppose she took a shine to him in any case and said he could stay in the lodgings in exchange for teaching some lessons. And that's what he did, when he wasn't going around all the different claims looking for someone to agree to his research project.

One of the other teachers was a fellow by the name of Bartholomew Hunter, who helped Heck to understand the school and the town as well. Of

African descent as well. But like Heck, he also wasn't a local fellow. He was actually from the United States—Louisiana, I think it was. His parents had bought their freedom sometime earlier, so he had grown up free where many like him were still slaves. This young man hated slavery, the idea of slavery, everything about it—and no surprise, it's a terrible thing. His parents told him how they had suffered. It's strange to think of it now, but he had come to the Cape because he'd heard it was an example to the world—and especially America—for how the races could live in harmony as equals.

Now, the Union of South Africa is not an equal place. Whatever that poor young man was hoping to learn, the country demonstrated the opposite. But from the time the Cape Colony was founded until about twenty years ago, any man with twenty-five pounds to his name and the ability to read had a vote, be he black, white, Indian, or whatever else. This would've been the Cape that the young Mr. Hunter wanted to see.

This Mr. Hunter had strong opinions about the equality of his people among all others, and those were not so popular with everyone he met. He'd argue with people, they'd end up getting in accidents—which was common enough—and he'd be blamed for it, no matter how long ago the argument had been. He had made an enemy of two brothers, Hubert and Basil. Like Heck, they were young British men. They had arrived in New Rush only a little before Heck, but they'd quickly gained influence amongst the diamond miners. They even held a few claims of their own.

It might have been easy for Heck to distance himself from this Hunter fellow, but all the same, they became close friends. Perhaps because they were so unlike one another. Hunter loved spectacle and show business and putting on magic tricks for the schoolchildren. Heck, at the time, only cared for science and thought magic was ridiculous. He says they made friends when they argued about it. You can picture it, can't you?

'You want to come see my magic show?'

'Bah, magic is all hokum,' says Heck. 'I'm not interested.'

'How can you say that without even seeing it?'

'Magic is the enemy of science, and science is the most important thing in the world.'

'How about this: you come and see my show, and if you can figure out how the magic is done—scientifically—I'll introduce you to some mine-owner friends?'

Of course, the truth about prestidigitation and illusion is that everything is scientific, just with misdirection to make it seem like magic. In the end, Heck found the show rather charming. He and this Mr. Hunter ended up thick as thieves, if you'll pardon the expression, and they took pride in teaching at the school together.

Now, Heck being Heck, he didn't sleep much and would go out on patrols at night. One day, he noticed that some of the children who slept in the school lodgings were sneaking out. He woke up Hunter, and the two of them went to town to see what the children were up to. They followed the children to one of the local taverns, where the students waited for someone who had insulted Mr. Hunter, tripping the man so that he fell into the horse trough. Schoolchildren, taking revenge for the slights directed at Mr. Hunter. Heck and Mr. Hunter helped the man, of course, but he only took a swing at Hunter in return—though it was probably easy enough to dodge.

The experience awakened something in Heck. Even though he and Mr. Hunter told off the children and made them promise they wouldn't do it again,

Heck knew they would. He began to patrol the town at night, stopping fights, rescuing the drunkards who fell into holes, and trying to help the many, many people injured in the mines. I'm sure he learned a thing or two back then that he's teaching you now.

Disaster struck during a night such as that. The two brothers, Hubert and Basil, had quarreled with Mr. Hunter and left him in a very sore mood. When the children found out about it, they decided to take revenge. They went to one of the brothers' mines, meaning to break the machines they found there. They probably hated the mines—friends and relatives, maybe even parents, went down into those pits and didn't come back. So a little gang of four or five children arrived with destruction in their hearts, and though they may have been just children, a determined child can pull apart even the most robust machine.

On this day, though, the schoolchildren were unlucky. Perhaps one of them simply hit the wrong part with a wrench, or perhaps Heck interrupted them, or perhaps one of the brothers or their men had set a trap. But a boy got his shirt tangled up in the moving parts of one of the machines, and it was pulling him in, where he would be certain to meet his end amongst the cogs and gears. Luckily, Heck had followed them.

You can picture him, can't you? Walking in and seeing this scene—'What the devil have you done?' Well, the drilling machine or whatever contraption it may have been, it was already in motion by then. Heck had to put his hands right into the whirring gears to free the lad. So that's what he did. He wrenched the boy free, and, well, it's probably no surprise to hear he spent the next few days in the hospital and never could quite move his left hand the same.

So there you have it. The story of Heck in the Cape Colony. From what I know, after that, he just focused on the reason he went in the first place. He concentrated on his research, wrote the paper he was there to write, and once he left, well, from what I know, he never looked back."

IX
A Bargain

U ncle Reggie's story had given me a lot to think about, but it didn't explain what had left Mr. Scant acting so strangely or what Aurelian knew about this time in my mentor's life. And there was no time to stop to think about it.

When Dr. Mikolaitis took me home, I found Mr. Jackdaw waiting for me. It was a strange scene—Mother receiving Mr. Jackdaw in the living room, where they sat having tea. Father was out on business, but evidently he had asked his valet to stay at home, so Mr. Scant stood at the side of the room in butler mode. Mrs. Winton, the kind old woman who was Mother's lady's maid as well as the housekeeper, sat on her little wooden chair by the door in case Mother needed her. While not as old as Mrs. Twiggs, Mrs. Winton was too old to stand too much these days, and normally she sat by Mother. But of course that wasn't the done thing while the house had company.

Mr. Jackdaw had made himself quite at home and was praising Mother for her taste in curtains.

"This must be your son," he said, standing up to greet me. His act of never having seen me before was once again remarkably convincing, and I could see no trace of his leg injury in the way he walked. "Oh, he looks much more like you than like Sandleforth. Good day to you, young man. My name is Mr. Pouncey. My company works with your father's."

"Nice to meet you," I said, making sure Mother couldn't see how I glared at him as I stepped forward to shake his hand. "My name is Oliver."

"What a pleasure. *Argh!* Quite a firm handshake you have there, my boy."

I smiled sweetly and thanked him as he cradled his hand, though I was fairly sure he was just humoring me.

Mr. Jackdaw turned back to my mother. "Well, I shouldn't take up any more of your time, but thank you so much for the tea and the scone. I'll call on your husband at his factory."

"It was my pleasure."

Mr. Scant left with Mr. Jackdaw, ostensibly to fetch our visitor's coat and hat for him. It would have seemed strange for me to go with them, so I sat with Mother.

"Did they announce the fencing team members?" she asked.

"Not yet. I think it usually takes a few days."

"I'm pleased you've decided you like fencing. When I was a nurse, we had one patient who had the most terrible neck injury from his time as a scrum-half. He was only twenty and he never walked again. Just for a ball game. It did make me worry, when you were playing rugby so much."

"You don't have to worry about me."

"What a big, tough rabbit!"

All of a sudden, she grabbed me and pulled me toward her for a big hug.

"Gah! Stop, stop, stop!"

"Not tough enough to escape me yet," she said, cackling as Mrs. Winton shook her head and took out her knitting.

When I managed to extricate myself, I claimed I had schoolwork to do and took my leave. I did have schoolwork, but it could wait, because Mr. Jackdaw had clearly come to see Mr. Scant—and no doubt me as well. I hurried to the Ice House. Inside, I found Mr. Jackdaw looking flustered.

"I don't think you're taking this seriously enough," he was saying. "I've had to work my fingers to the bone just to stop this from becoming an international incident. We let multiple visiting police force representatives get shot."

"*You* let them get shot," said Mr. Scant. "I was there as a guest. And so you could hold me up like some sort of trophy. Me and the boy."

He met my eye as I made my way down the stairs to join them at the bottom of the big underground space. The huge brick cylinder that was the Ice House always made me feel as though I had been shrunk down and dropped into the kind of jar people put butterflies into. The whole place still smelt vaguely of ash from the time the Woodhouselee Society had come to destroy it. Mr. Scant looked troubled and distracted—a subtle change from his usual surliness, but I knew him well enough that it was obvious to me.

"The wretched Binns boy made a threat that we cannot just ignore," Mr. Jackdaw said. "This is a direct consequence of your deposing his father, and I would thank you to take some responsibility."

"No," said Mr. Scant. "It's none of our concern. I didn't stop Roland Binns because he once stole the sword from the Crown Jewels. I stopped Binns because he made *my brother* do it for him. It was a family matter."

"He shot at you. Surely that makes it personal enough?"

"Many people have shot at me in my time. It never worried me unduly."

Only then did Mr. Jackdaw see me. He held up a hand beseechingly. "Ollie! Ollie, please help me talk some sense into him!"

"What's this about?" I asked.

"Apparently," Mr. Scant said, "it's our duty to stop that boy from stealing the sceptre and its diamond, regardless of the risks. Well, I'll tell you, I'm against it."

"What do you expect us to do?" I asked Mr. Jackdaw.

"Who else has already studied the security measures of the Tower of London's Jewel House? Who better to think like a thief than the famous Ruminating Claw himself?"

Mr. Scant bristled, but I held up a hand. "Mr. Scant wasn't a thief. He only ever took what had already been stolen and put it back where it belonged. And I won't be any help. This business with the sword happened before I became Mr. Scant's apprentice."

"All right, yes, I take back 'thief.' But Scant still broke into the Jewel House, despite the many precautions in place. His advice is invaluable."

"My advice is to flood the place with guards," said Mr. Scant. "You have men, don't you? Just make sure there's a round-the-clock guard with dozens of men from the Yard."

"Of course that was my first thought," Mr. Jackdaw said. "But this whole affair is still confidential. To get that kind of manpower, we'd need an official report about what happened, and Sir Frederickson still wants it kept hush-hush. Now, I can't tell you why that is, but it's not my place to question. And besides . . ."

His voice trailed off.

"Besides what?" I asked.

Mr. Jackdaw looked uncharacteristically rueful for a moment. Then his false smile returned. "Besides, I pledged to deal with it myself."

Mr. Scant shook his head. "Arrogance."

"The truth is, I need help," said Mr. Jackdaw. "If I don't sort this out, my head will be on the block. I don't want to lose this job. I've given up my life for it. In fact, giving up my life was the minimum requirement. You wouldn't believe what I've sacrificed, so . . . I'm sorry if it was arrogant, but I'm asking you, *please*, will you help me?"

I looked to Mr. Scant, who was looking at the floor. After a while, he sighed, and to my surprise it was me he addressed.

"This man is a manipulator. We have no reason to trust anything he says. If I say I will not help, my concern is that he will convince you to assist him anyway. And I won't be able to protect you."

"Why does everyone think I need protecting?" I said, and in that moment, I saw Mr. Jackdaw sit up just a little. "That doesn't mean I'm going to go," I told him.

Mr. Jackdaw's perfectly white teeth reappeared. "Of course."

"I think it's a matter of weighing up the pros and cons," I reasoned. "If we don't help, Aurelian takes the diamond, sells it, and then he has the money to make his—what was it?—his Third Day Society. If we help, maybe we stop him."

"Or maybe we end up dead," said Mr. Scant.

"I thought people shooting at you never worried you?"

Mr. Scant sighed. "We don't even know when he's planning to strike. We can't guard the jewels indefinitely."

"Nor would I ask you to," said Mr. Jackdaw. "The plan isn't to guard the sceptre. The plan is to steal it before he does. We leave at six o'clock tomorrow morning—be ready."

X

The Tower

"**T**his is ridiculous," Mr. Scant said.

I shifted uncomfortably. To enter the Tower of London, Mr. Jackdaw had disguised us with the red uniforms of the tower's guards, the Yeomen Warders—better known as the Beefeaters. The outfits were ostentatious, all red with gold embroidery, not to mention a stiff ruff at the neck and tunics that went down to the knees. Mr. Scant had refused to put on the shoes, which were topped with flowery rosettes.

"Firstly, this isn't even the everyday Beefeater uniform," he said. "This is their *ceremonial* outfit, so it's meaningless for us to wear it. Secondly, these are old uniforms, still embroidered with *V.R.* for Her Majesty Queen Victoria, may she rest in peace. And thirdly, warders have to be retired military men who have served more than twenty-two years. How does a fourteen-year-old boy qualify?"

"You're not in disguise from the Beefeaters themselves," Mr. Jackdaw said, smiling politely. "You are in disguise from the public, so no citizens presume to stop you once you're in the Jewel House. The warders know who you are and why you're here. Well, not the entirety of who you are, but they know you're here on my behalf. They think you're agents of the yard."

"You've been telling people that an awful lot," said Mr. Scant.

"If you spoke to the warders already," I said, "why do we need to be here? Can't you just get them to give the sceptre to you?"

"The warders can't be the ones to take the sceptre out. They can turn a blind eye but they're not going to do the deed themselves. And while the Yard may be able to persuade a handful of Beefeaters to help, the Keeper of the Jewels, General Wynne, is another matter. Whatever alliance we have here, it falls apart if he gets word of this."

"You didn't answer the boy's question," said Mr. Scant. "They can't get the sceptre out, but you could do it just as easily as me. Perhaps you just need someone to blame if the effort goes sour?"

"If this goes belly-up, I can do all the blaming I like, but it's still my head on the chopping block. *You* I need because you know how to get into the case containing the jewels quickly and efficiently and you can react swiftly if anything unexpected happens, what?"

"You understand," said Mr. Scant, "that last time, I filled the room with smoke and then descended by way of a rope?"

"I don't think that will be necessary. Although I was unable to procure the keys you'll need—and believe me, I tried—so I'm rather hoping your famous prowess with the lock picks will come in handy."

I pulled on my flowery hat. "Come on, Mr. Scant. We're here now. What's the harm in us helping out?"

"I'd rather we didn't have to play dress-up," Mr. Scant said, but he pulled on his own hat nonetheless.

We had met at the Tower of London, inside the White Tower itself, in rooms not normally open to the public. This way, we could discuss our plans away from any tourist who might have overheard. The jewels were in another building, one of the many towers making up the outer wall. Though the tower in question was connected to the Bloody Tower and stood just across from Traitors' Gate, it had the disappointingly ordinary name of Wakefield Tower.

As we made our way there, I couldn't help but feel a sense of excitement. The whole fortress complex was a daunting place, with gray stone walls that seemed to forbid any kind of enjoyment, and yet this was so far one of the more enjoyable things I had ever done. And I certainly preferred wearing strange clothes for a clandestine mission with the full permission of Scotland Yard to groping around in a cave in Hastings.

There were a great number of tourists visiting the Wakefield Tower, and several of them looked over to us, no doubt curious to see what two Beefeaters were doing in ceremonial dress. Perhaps they also wondered why one was so much shorter than the other. I comforted myself with the thought that it can't have been so very unusual. After all, this uniform had presumably once belonged to a real warder, and it was only a little too big for me.

I had been given a plump velvet cushion to carry, the plan being for Mr. Scant to take out the sceptre, then for me to carry it out of the room with great pomp and circumstance. Later, our allies among the warders would take back a replica, which would serve until Aurelian missed his sale. Ideally he would see that the sceptre had been replaced and give up, but if he stole the replica and didn't realize his error until attempting to pass off the forgery, that would also be well and good. Mr. Jackdaw had prepared a second replica in case this happened.

My excitement turned to embarrassment when we reached the entranceway to the upper chamber of the tower and a real Yeoman Warder in a black uniform looked me up and down with an eyebrow raised. Somewhere, one of the famous ravens cawed, as if the bird were laughing at me on the man's behalf. I pulled the hat down over my face a little, then followed Mr. Scant into the Jewel House.

The room was quite a marvel. Under a high vaulted ceiling with a dozen arches was a huge glass case. Bright electric light illuminated its contents, and sturdy iron railings encased them all around. At the top were numerous spikes—wrought to look artful, but they remained as sharp and dangerous-looking as could be, like a deadly echo of crowns and tiaras. Inside the case sparkled the Crown Jewels, considerably bigger than I expected. The crown itself stood resplendent at the top, and a whole host of orbs and sceptres surrounded it in tiers, like some great wedding cake frosted in gold and jewels.

The half-dozen tourists viewing the display turned to look at us as we came in. Mr. Jackdaw shifted away, then swiveled back curiously, as though he were simply another tourist who had happened to come in at the same time as two Beefeaters. Holding up the velvet cushion like a ring-bearer at a wedding, I followed Mr. Scant.

The remarkable thing about our theft was how unremarkable it was. Mr. Scant picked the lock to the sceptre's cage with a skill I could only aspire to match. He didn't need to kneel down or peer at his handiwork. If I hadn't known better, he would have appeared simply to be using a key with a rather stubborn lock. Then the door was open, and he stepped inside.

I wasn't sure exactly what happened next. I was keeping my head low in case someone's curiosity about why I was so much younger than the other warders got the better of them, so I couldn't tell exactly how Mr. Scant got to the sceptre itself. But after what seemed like several minutes, he returned, placed the sceptre onto the cushion, and slowly locked the cage door behind him. During this time, I marveled at the object I was holding. It was much longer than I expected it to be, overhanging the cushion on both sides, almost as long as my fencing swords. At the end was the diamond Aurelian meant to steal, the Star of Africa. Tiny rainbows appeared with every minute movement I made, sparking for a moment and then vanishing again.

Mr. Scant began walking, so I walked along behind him. Although tourists had continued watching us, as I could see from the corners of my eyes, they simply stood aside reverentially.

As we passed through the jewel room doorway, I felt my excitement building. There was a priceless symbol of the power of the king in my hands. Out in the open, with nothing else protecting it, only me. Mr. Scant and I could certainly deal with anyone who had managed to get close. But if Aurelian were inside the Wakefield Tower, and he were able to sneak up without my noticing, he could have taken it right from me.

It was a thought that stung a little when Aurelian did precisely that.

XI
Gray

I had been so intent on avoiding the eyes of tourists and keeping the priceless crown jewel balanced that I had no idea from where Aurelian appeared. But he was there, blocking our way to the stairs that lead down from the Jewel House. In an instant he stepped forward to take the Sceptre with Cross.

Somewhere in my mind I'd expected this to happen, so I dropped the cushion and tried to wrench it from his grasp. Throughout all this, the main thing running through my head was that the lumps I was pulling on were probably jewels that cost more than all Father's factories.

In every scenario I had imagined, this would be as much as I would have to struggle, because Mr. Scant would intervene. But instead, the man once feared throughout England as a master criminal just stood there, looking away from us.

Aurelian smiled a cruel smile and leaned closer to me. "Oliver Diplexito," he said, intoning every syllable of my surname as if they formed the lines of a poem. "For what you did to my family, you're going to live a long life, full of suffering."

All I could think to say was, "Let go!"

I pulled as hard as I could on the sceptre, but Aurelian was bigger and stronger than me. "I'll never let you take it," I said, with what I hoped was a determined look.

"I can think of many enjoyable ways to make you," Aurelian said, "but mostly I want to see your face when I do *this*."

He used his free hand to press something on the sceptre, and the three metal arcs that held the diamond in place loosened, opening like flower petals in the sun. The great diamond came unstuck, and with a small twist, Aurelian had it out of the sceptre altogether. He not only released his grip but used the sceptre to give me a shove.

"Mr. Scant!" I called as I stumbled back, but there was no response. Mr. Scant seemed to be frozen in place. Then Aurelian was upon me again, grabbing me by the collar of the uniform that seemed such an absurd thing to be wearing now.

"I wanted to try this just once," he said as he held up the glistening, magnificent diamond. He closed his fist around it and swung it hard into my gut.

I felt all the air pushed out of me. Then the pain set in. Before I knew it, I was on the floor, gasping for breath. Aurelian sneered at me for a moment before turning away. Though my vision blurred, I watched as he put his hand around Mr. Scant's shoulders, holding up the Star of Africa before him. That seemed to shake Mr. Scant out of whatever trance he was in. He made a grab for the jewel, but Aurelian was ready and danced away, laughing.

Then someone else was surging up the stairs and shoving Mr. Scant with all his strength. The attacker was a very tall man in a bulky winter coat, with dark skin and short white hair. My vision cleared enough for me to see his fiery eyes as he pushed Mr. Scant against the wall.

"Fly away home, Gray," he said in a rumbling American accent. The man took the diamond from Aurelian to hold in front of Mr. Scant's face. "This is coming with me. To where it belongs. Fly away home and stay out of this."

Mr. Scant was in no position to respond. Aurelian let out a derisive laugh.

"Stay out of this," the tall man repeated, and let Mr. Scant drop. Then he and Aurelian turned away to descend the stairs.

Mr. Scant didn't move, even when I groaned. After a time, I managed to roll over and get up on my hands and knees. Before me was the Sceptre with Cross, bereft of its diamond, where I had dropped it.

"Why didn't you stop them?" I wheezed. Mr. Scant only shook his head. He was pale and looked for all the world like a confused old man. It was not an expression I'd seen before and it scared me. I forced myself to get up and chase after Aurelian but I could still barely breathe. I almost tripped down the stairs, saving myself only by falling against the wall instead. The men were already gone.

We said nothing more until Mr. Jackdaw came dashing up the stairs. His clothes were torn and he held one hand to a new wound on his shoulder. His usual smile was absent.

"Report," he said. "What happened?"

"They took it," I said, handing over the sceptre, which Mr. Jackdaw regarded as though it were a poisonous snake.

"Why didn't you fight? That's what you're here for, isn't it?"

"I thought we were here to take the diamond while you made sure nobody was coming," I said.

"Yes, well . . . ," Mr. Jackdaw said. He began to inspect the sceptre as though perhaps the huge diamond were hidden somewhere just out of sight. "I had hoped you would be a capable enough fighter to keep this from happening," he said to Mr. Scant. "I thought that was your specialty."

Mr. Scant stared at the floor. I wasn't sure he even heard what Mr. Jackdaw said.

"They caught us by surprise," I said. "And Mr. Scant didn't—" I stopped myself and reconsidered. "We couldn't stop them."

Mr. Jackdaw's lips moved as though he were performing a difficult calculation. Then he softened. "Are you hurt?" he asked, looking at the hand I'd wrapped around my belly.

"A little," I said. "He got me pretty good. Aurelian."

"Who was the other chap?"

"Someone strong," was all I could say.

"Here's what we're going to do," Mr. Jackdaw said. "We're going to get that diamond back. We're going to stop it from getting sold and we're going to put it back here where it belongs. And we're going to do it without anybody else knowing. Agreed? My final report will say that this was a great success, with only a small delay, and we're going to make sure that it is. Otherwise, since you two took the jewel out of its case, officially speaking, you're the ones who stole it. I'm sure you understand. Now then—I was not entirely unprepared for this eventuality . . ."

From his inner pocket he produced another diamond—no, not a diamond, but in fact a large piece of glass, carved to look like the Star of Africa. He put the false Star into the sceptre and fixed the clasps around it. Then he picked up the pillow and held it out to me.

"You two put it back where it was. Then I'll take you both home and we'll figure out a solution that won't get us executed."

Throughout the journey home, Mr. Scant continued to act like a scolded child. He wouldn't meet my eye and mostly stared at his hands. I tried to say encouraging things like, "There was nothing we could have done," and, "Next time we'll make better plans."

Each time, he pretended he couldn't hear me.

It was almost enough to make me lose my temper. So I said something I knew would provoke a reaction.

"That was Mr. Hunter, wasn't it?"

As expected, Mr. Scant looked at me in surprise. "How do you know that name?" he said, his voice barely a whisper.

"Uncle Reggie told me about him. I asked him when I saw that photo Aurelian gave you. I thought Mr. Hunter wanted to be a hero. Didn't seem like much of a hero to me."

"He *is* a hero," Mr. Scant said with sudden venom. "What did Reggie tell you?"

"Well . . . he told me you went to Africa. To the Cape Colony, and you stayed at a school. Miss Handle's school. And how you hurt your hands when you saved a boy in the mines. He said you and Mr. Hunter wanted to be heroes and help people."

"Reggie likes to tell stories," muttered Mr. Scant. "Usually he doesn't know what he's talking about. I expect he used all sorts of stupid voices . . ."

"Well, he did try."

Mr. Scant sighed. "Better you know the truth of the matter than some half-truth. Hunter absolutely was a hero. We called him, 'Hunter the Just,' because it sounded like the hero in some old story of knights and princesses. And he was my teacher. My teacher in all things. I suppose I had better tell you what really happened."

XII
Mr. Scant's Story

"I was so young when I arrived at New Rush. Or Kimberley, as they call it today. Like most young men, I thought I knew everything and would live forever. I thought that I was so different from all the other young men arriving at the Cape Colony because I wasn't chasing after diamonds to get rich. Now I know they all thought they were different and special, in their own way.

In New Rush, you couldn't rely on the police or governors or judges. The first thing I did was get myself conned out of most of my money. You'd think, in a place like that, cutthroats and bandits wouldn't last long. Everyone knows everyone, and if a man would slit your throat for the shirt on your back, he's a danger to all the rest. And it's true—the violent types were quickly taken care of. But the ones who would smile at you and tell you they needed to check your papers—for administrative purposes, of course—and then fool you into handing over your money, well, they thrived there. They weren't causing trouble. The ones they duped were just fools. And a fool I was.

And that's where I met Hunter. 'Up to your old tricks, gents?' That's the first thing I heard him say. The con men told him to go away, in somewhat more vulgar language. But he shook his head. 'You took something from my friend here that doesn't belong to you. Let's have it back.'

'It's three on one this time,' said one of the men. 'You can't beat us all.'

'A hero never backs down from a fight.' That's what he said.

A common man as a hero—not such a wild idea now, but back then the image of a hero was a king or a general. Hunter didn't care about that. He was a man who would come to help a complete stranger and was willing to get hurt in doing so. And he did get hurt. Those three men got in a few jabs, maybe cut his cheek a little bit, but they weren't fighters. Hunter was a fighter. A born fighter, who had grown up fighting for his life. It was a small thing for him, to take care of three men and send them running.

Of course, I was grateful, but he only doffed his cap and smiled before disappearing. We didn't meet again until I found a job working at a school for local children. The proprietor there was one Miss Nosuthu Handle, a very handsome young woman who had offered me lodgings when there were no others to be found. Her school accepted any child who wished to learn. Children of Khoi farmers who had worked the nearby lands since time immemorial. Children of the Bantu peoples, whose ancestors came from the north. Young Indian children whose parents had grown sugarcane to the east of us. All were welcome. Often I was told I should not teach in such a place, but I never listened. It became my home, and I loved it.

Working as a teacher suited me well. It gave me good reasons to connect with the town's scientific community, such as it was. Rather to my surprise, Hunter was working there too. While I taught mathematics and the sciences, Hunter the Just was in charge of literature and classics. Though we had to intervene when he decided to teach nothing but heroic epics.

I didn't have the easiest time in New Rush. Diamonds were jealously protected, and nobody there cared about studying the material properties of what they unearthed, only how much it would sell for when cut and polished. I went all over town, snatching a meeting here, a short examination of tiny diamonds there, though I was quite content even with that.

However, in New Rush, everybody had an enemy. Smile at one man and you make an enemy of another. Some of them thought I was too clever. Some of them thought I should only associate with other whites. And some of them had been beaten by Hunter. They resented him but found him a difficult target. It wasn't uncommon to notice some hostile party following me during an errand. I learned to walk silently, to listen for the footsteps behind me, but that wasn't always enough. Sometimes they cornered me and beat me just to laugh at me.

Hunter soon caught wind of this, but I refused his help. I thought it was shameful, to be pitied. That changed at breakfast one day, when Miss Handle asked me about my future plans. I told her that I was obliged to join the navy upon my return to England.

'The military?' Hunter said. 'You're going to get eaten alive.'

'I hope to focus on science there,' I said.

'Always science with you,' he replied. 'You still have to get through basic training. You're gonna die.'

'You almost sound as though you'd like to help me,' I said.

'Just a warning,' he said. He knew that if he offered, I would be too proud to accept. 'I guess I could use you as a sparring partner. But that's for *my* benefit.'

Hunter was what we call a vigilante. In his heart he wanted a peaceful world, free of danger, but his way toward that was violence. You probably wouldn't believe me if I told you I didn't believe in violence then. But I came to believe that the threat of force might really be all that keeps bad people from making victims of the weak. So I joined Hunter on his patrols.

When there was nothing to do, he trained me. Trained me to be fit, to be fast. Lessons that stuck with me for life. I would follow him, but where he liked to be loud and brash, I liked to be silent. He called me 'Gray Owl' because of how quietly I could move. We would stop robberies, break up fights, protect the vulnerable new arrivals, rescue cats from trees—that sort of thing. Small works, but we were proud. And I worked hard, wanting to be as good as him. Maybe even better.

The more we did it, the more we believed in ourselves. If I was a gray owl, he was a bald eagle. He loved spectacle and bombast—very American—whereas I took advantage of his distractions. We even took to fighting with claws on our hands. Hunter had read about warrior monks fighting in the style of animals. Though we had no inkling of how those monks actually fought, as an eagle and an owl, we found it a fine inspiration.

He made me teach him to make firecrackers and smoke bombs, until at times I worried our peace-keeping had become a show. Magic—he was always a fan of magic. Of course, illusion is just science plus deception, but for him the deception was crucial and the science more of a shameful secret. We fought over that many a time, though never seriously. The kind of fight that lets you know you have a true friend. Of course, our little imaginary world couldn't last forever. One day we found some men beating the owner of a small mine—a place, or claim, where only one diamond had ever been found, months earlier. Hunter and I intervened, and afterward, the owner tried to reward us with the deed to his mine.

Out of gratitude, though I suspect he was also growing tired of the dangers of New Rush.

'I can't accept it,' Hunter said, 'but you can give it to the school.'

A noble gesture, but that was the beginning of the end for us. I was happy because the deed gave me a direct connection to the diamonds, allowing me to write my papers. For Hunter, it was more than that. A group of black and mixed-race business owners had helped Miss Handle found her school. To own a mine as well—this was a symbol of progress, of their growing influence.

But the diamond business was cutthroat. Certain men wanted a monopoly. They were angry at those of us who pushed back against the coercion, the beatings. They were angry because they couldn't beat us, and the Hero of New Rush was becoming too popular for them to slander. And so they took the children from us. Four of them, in the night, from their beds in the school. They offered us a simple deal—sign over the rights to the mines or they would end the children's lives.

Such was life in New Rush. Still, we were fighters, and we were flush with arrogance. We thought we were invincible, and honestly, there was nobody who would compare to us in a fair fight. But that's why nobody pictured a fair fight.

Hunter and I went to the mine where the children were being held, armed with our fireworks and our smoke, convinced nobody could stop up. And of course we came up against a hired mob armed with knives, guns, clubs. There were more of them than there were of us, and yet we thought it was all a bluff. No one would hurt the children. Not really. 'Just you try it,' I remember Hunter saying. 'See what happens if you harm one hair on their heads.'

Only this man, Hubert Fields, he wasn't bluffing. He was what you might call genuinely evil. One of the Englishmen who believe that a drop of black blood makes you somehow less human. Less worthy of life. There were, and still are, many of those.

Hubert enjoyed showing off his wealth, and inside his mine he had a large combustion engine. A great machine with a furnace that drove great big wheels around and around. It was meant to move large belts that pulled things out of the mine. And he had one student, this lad named Samson, with his wrists tied to the belt. All he had to do was pull down a lever and it would draw the boy into the machine, into these great big wheels. The three other children were tied in the same way, their wrists tied to Samson's so that they would follow one by one. All for show, I thought. A grand gesture.

'I'll deal with Fields,' I said to Hunter. 'You keep his men off me.'

I truly thought it would be that simple. Well, Hubert saw me coming for him and shot at me, but he took so long about it that I had no trouble finding some cover. But that's where I made my mistake.

'Let the children go, Hubert,' I called out to him. 'You're not a monster, you're an Englishman. It's not in you to hurt another human being.'

I really believed that would be the end of it. Only Hubert was more monster than I could have ever guessed. As if to prove me wrong, he pulled down that lever and set the machine in motion. Perhaps he assumed I would be able to stop it. I can't be certain. But that machine moved so very fast, it was only a second, maybe two, before the boy's hands would be crushed between the two wheels.

The only thing I could think to do was jam something metal between those moving parts, to stop up the wheels. And the only metal object within reach was the claw on my left hand, made of kitchen knives and broken mining tools I'd put together. There wasn't time for anything else.

It didn't work exactly as I'd hoped. The claw was crushed around my hand, taking most of the skin with it. But the machine stopped long enough for me to pull loose one of the blades in my other hand and cut loose the ropes, freeing young Samson. By then my left hand was being pulled ever more into the machine, and I had to pull myself free with the right. In the end I lost most of the skin from both hands in the effort.

I'm not sure exactly what happened after that. My memories are confused. The fighting stopped, presumably when hired hands realized this was more than they had been paid for. I remember at the end it was only me and Hunter and the crying children. Alone with the results of our arrogance.

In the days afterward, I poured myself into writing my papers. I refused to see Hunter when he came to talk. It's the only time I turned my back on someone in need. But I was too frightened we might put the children in danger again.

Hunter seemed to abandon his hero idea, or at least the idea of being a vigilante. I always imagined him continuing his fight through a thing like politics. If he did, he was on the losing side.

Nobody arrested Hubert. Though a few years later, he went wandering around Lake Nyasa and was one day found dead from a bullet wound. They called it a shooting accident. I never cared to investigate.

But Hubert's brother, Basil, became a rich and powerful man. Basil Fields always worked to take away the rights of people like Hunter, to take away all the freedoms that had attracted Hunter in the first place. I regret not staying to help, but in a way, I no longer believed I could. I left New Rush without saying goodbye to its fallen hero. I never thought I would see him again.

I completed my basic training with the Royal Navy, thanks in no small part to what I learned from Hunter, and was a junior science officer for about five years, from 1874 on. But when I heard a new war might be coming in South Africa, I pictured being sent there on a combat ship and I couldn't abide the idea. I retired from the navy to attend university, and never set foot in the Cape Colony again."

XIII
A Note to the Headmaster

T he next day was a Sunday. I half-expected Mr. Jackdaw to be waiting for us at church, but the day passed uneventfully. I thought about going to talk to Mr. Scant again, but he kept his distance from me, and I could sense that telling me that story had exhausted him. It rained all day, so I mostly stayed indoors, reading my detective novel and watching the rain fall on the twisted thorny twigs that would soon transform into Mother's roses.

On Monday, the results of the fencing trial were posted on the Judner's School notice board. My name was there, but not where I'd been hoping for. I found it under *Team Reserve Members*. In fact, the main team hadn't changed at all.

Chudley clapped his hands on my shoulders. "You made it!"

"Onto the reserves," I said. "Reserves never do anything."

"You only started a few months ago!" Chudley said, incredulous. "And we're second years. All these, they're all fourth and fifth years. What, did you expect to be team captain already?"

"Not *captain*," I mumbled.

"Cheer up," he said. "Tell you what, I'll get you something from the tuck shop. How does an iced bun sound?"

"It's only nine in the morning," I said.

"That's why it's a treat."

"We don't have time before morning assembly."

"So we'll sneak them in."

"Will they even have iced buns in the morning?"

"Let's find out."

So that's what we did. There were no cakes on display at the tuck shop, but when we asked the shopkeeper—whose real name nobody knew—she said they had been delivered but she hadn't got them out yet. Chudley pleaded with her, saying we had a special event to celebrate, and she eventually conceded.

This is how we found ourselves smuggling buns into assembly. We waited until the headmaster began his droning morning talk before we started to sneak our first mouthfuls, and within moments we were drawing envious looks from all around us. Soon both Chudley and I were trying to stop ourselves from laughing, our fingers covered in sticky icing.

Of course, one of the prefects stopped us outside assembly, hurling accusations, but I said, "Can you prove it?" Flustered, he told us not to do it again.

After a week of escaping a burning building, failing to prevent the theft of a priceless diamond, and hearing Mr. Scant tell a harrowing story from his past, a day at school learning about Pythagoras or vocative plurals felt like a holiday.

At lunchtime, Chudley and I found ourselves staring at our lunchboxes without much enthusiasm.

"I'm still full from the iced bun," I said.

"Me too," said Chudley. "Though I quite fancy another bun, actually."

We met one another's eye, and no more needed to be said. The shop's lady gave us a disapproving look when we bought our third and fourth iced buns of the day, but she made no comment.

We returned to our seats in the dining hall to discover someone had stolen the fruits from our lunchboxes, which suited us just fine.

"Good riddance, banana," said Chudley.

"Good riddance, Granny Smith," I said. "Wait, isn't your family business something to do with fruit?"

"Imports. That's why I've had more than enough of it for one lifetime," Chudley said, regarding his iced bun as though it were a bar of solid gold. "The worst part is when there's a whole crate of stuff that wouldn't sell. We have to eat it before it goes rotten."

"Where does the company buy the fruit from?" I asked. "Anything from Africa?"

"Africa, India, Brazil. All sorts of places," he said.

"Have you ever met someone from Africa?"

"Sure. Why do you ask?"

"I met someone the other day," I said. "Oh, actually, no, that's wrong. He was from America, but he lives in Africa. And I suppose his family came from Africa. His ancestors, I mean."

"One of my great aunts married a doctor from Morocco," Chudley said. "He's so funny. He always has a joke for anything you can think of. Though I remember he got angry once because he was reading an article in the newspaper. It called people from Africa 'barbarians.' He said the people around the Mediterranean Sea have more in common with each other than they do with people from England. So Rome's more like Casablanca than London. Hadn't thought of that. We know people from England and Scotland are different, so why do we think all of Africa is just the same? I don't suppose all of Morocco is the same, even."

"That makes sense," I said. "My tutor is from Lithuania. It's part of Russia, but he gets angry if you say, 'Lithuania, *in Russia*.' He wants it to become its own country again. Even in one place, you get a lot of different history."

That gave me more to think about. I kept picturing the face of Mr. Hunter. I wondered what Aurelian had told him, to make him attack Mr. Scant, his old friend. Despite all that Mr. Scant had told me, I could think only of how much I didn't know.

After school, Mr. Jackdaw was waiting for me. He looked a little less polished than usual, with his moustache a little disheveled and dark circles under his eyes. He kept his practiced smile, though, as he doffed his hat to me.

"Who's that?" said Chudley. "He looks suspicious."

"Oh, uh—he's a Diplexito Engineering associate," I said. "Father must have sent him to pick me up. I'll see you tomorrow, okay?"

Mr. Jackdaw led me to a rather ostentatious motorcar, and we climbed into the back. After telling the driver to drive on, he let out a deep sigh.

"This is a pickle we're in and no mistaking it," he said. "We're on our own, Ollie, my boy. We have to get the Star back. It's imperative. I'm not up in front of the firing squad just yet, but if we fail to find the diamond, it won't be long. I've been speaking with Mr. Scant, and he wants nothing to do with this. Do you think you can convince him?"

"Don't you think this has gone far enough, Mr. Jackdaw?" I said. "Wouldn't it be better to just come clean about the whole thing? Then you can have all the police officers you want to help catch Aurelian."

"It's not that simple," he said. "And I can't promise there will be no consequences for you, either."

"Me? What have I done?"

Mr. Jackdaw took out a small metal flask and took a drink from it. "Well, it was you who allowed the Binns boy to get his hands on the Star. You and Mr. Scant took it from where it belonged. Probably I can ensure that the blame falls solely on my head, but that's only a *probably*. I'm not in a position to give guarantees."

"Do I have a choice?"

He looked away immediately.

After a time, I asked, "What exactly has Mr. Scant said?"

"He doesn't want to see me," said Mr. Jackdaw. "All he told me is that he doesn't think he can help me. That he can't fight at all any more. Do you know why? Because I certainly don't."

"Not completely, but one of the men we saw at the Tower, he was . . . I think someone Mr. Scant knew when he was young. A friend or a kind of teacher. And now Mr. Scant's not himself."

"It's a problem. We need your mentor's talents."

"If I go, he'll come too. But I don't think he can fight like he usually does. Not now."

"You can," said Mr. Jackdaw. "You've learned a lot from him, Ollie."

"But I'm not like him. I'm just learning. I wasn't even good enough to get on the fencing team. I want to say I'm strong, but I'm not strong like Mr. Scant. Not even close."

Mr. Jackdaw sat back in frustration. "If only we had someone else on hand who could fight like that. I'd feel a lot better about our chances."

A thought came to my mind. "There is someone

I know. Someone strong like Mr. Scant. Here in Tunbridge Wells."

"You mean it? Who?"

"I'll show you." I tapped on the glass that separated us from the driver, and Mr. Jackdaw turned a handle that wound it down. "Can you take us to Monson Road?"

"Certainly, sir," said the driver. "What number?"

"I don't know the number," I said. "But it's a butcher's shop. Troughton's Butchers."

XIV
Matilda Troughton

"**W**elcome to Trought-*wurgh*!"

The Valkyrie looked at me aghast.

I nodded and gave her a little smile. Mr. Jackdaw stepped into the little butcher's shop after me and grabbed my arm, squeezing it tight. He stopped a moment later, pretending nothing had happened.

"Can we talk?" I asked her.

"I, er—is it something important?"

"Yes," I said.

"Well, then, I'll get Pa to cover for me and, erm, I suppose I had better change. One moment."

When she had slipped away though the door behind the counter, I turned to Mr. Jackdaw, but he continued staring forward, shaking his head.

"I know she's a bit terrifying," I said, "but—"

He looked at me with his eyes wide. "Who is that angel? I must say, that's the finest woman upon whom I've ever had the privilege to gaze."

"The *Valkyrie?*" I said. Matilda Troughton had clever eyes and a handsome sort of face, but she was so tall and muscular that I couldn't imagine any sculptor including her in his heavenly choir.

"*She's* the Valkyrie?" said Mr. Jackdaw. "I've read many reports about her. But I had no idea she was such a vision. And from everything I've read, she's a bright one too. Whatever is she doing in a place like this?"

"She's reformed," I said. "She doesn't do bad things any more. This is her family's business."

"I suppose that makes sense, what with the cleavers."

The Valkyrie reappeared alongside a surprisingly short man with a wide flat nose and a few strands of hair combed over the top of his head. He looked at us darkly as his daughter apologized for keeping us waiting.

"Shall we go upstairs?" she said, lifting a hinged section of the counter to let us through. "I've boiled some water for tea."

We stepped past cuts of meat lain out on the counter, prices scrawled on little cards by each one.

Like most butchers' shops, Troughton's was a grim and smelly place, with various cuts hanging up by the window in a way that always made me feel more queasy than peckish. I expected more of the same in the back room, or worse, but all we saw there was a neat desk for doing the accounts.

"She's a good girl, y'hear?" Mr. Troughton said, leaning back. "She's keeping 'erself out of trouble."

"I think so too," I said.

The Valkyrie led us up a narrow staircase that creaked loudly with every step. She had to twist her broad shoulders a little just to make her way up. Waiting for us at the top was a funny little room with all sorts of dainty little decorative plates and crocheted cloths on every surface. Most of the plates depicted kittens, puppies, or chubby-faced little children. A doll dressed like Little Bo Peep sat in the corner with its glass eyes slightly crossed, a darling little sheep with a bow tie on her lap. There was a lot of pink about.

An older woman who I presumed to be Mrs. Troughton—though she was slightly bigger than her husband—set a tea tray on the little table and then withdrew with a modest bow. The Valkyrie sat on a chair that seemed far too small for her and began arranging the flowery teacups to pour.

"Erm, Miss Troughton, this is Mr. Jackdaw," I said. "He's from Scotland Yard."

The Valkyrie dropped the little spoon she'd been putting onto a saucer. Then she covered her face with both hands. "Oh no," she said. "Have you come to take me away?"

In a flash, Mr. Jackdaw went down on one knee in front of her and took her hands in his. "Oh, my dear young lady, not at all. Not at all! Please set your mind at ease. No misfortune shall befall you on my account, rest assured of that!"

The Valkyrie looked down at him as though his head had fallen off. I suspected my expression was similar. After a moment of silence, I thought I had better try to clear things up.

"We actually, er . . . we're here to ask for your help."

"My help?" said the Valkyrie, pulling her hands free and absently rubbing them together. Mr. Jackdaw sat back, grinning wider than ever.

"Yes. The thing is, well, you remember Mr. Binns and the Woodhouselee Society?"

"Of course I do. Much as I might want to forget. Please believe me when I tell you I was a different person then."

"I . . . want to believe that," I said. "Now Mr.

Binns's son, Aurelian, has come back. He's gathering funds for a new Society in France. The Third Day, he calls it."

"You met him?"

"Yes. We tried to stop him stealing one of the Crown Jewels. But we didn't."

The Valkyrie handed us each a cup of tea. "Even with your Mr. Scant?"

I looked at Mr. Jackdaw nervously for a moment, then said, "That's what we've come to you for. Aurelian found someone, someone from Mr. Scant's past—and, well, I don't know all the details, but something's wrong, and Mr. Scant isn't fighting like he usually does. It's like he can't."

"So you . . . came to me?"

"You're the only one I know who could match him," I said.

"I haven't done any fighting for a year or more. Well, hardly any," she said uncomfortably. "I don't know if I can."

"I don't think you've forgotten. You're the Valkyrie, after all."

"No, Oliver. No. I'm just Tilly Troughton."

"All right, then," I said. "But you're still the strongest person I ever met."

The Valkyrie chewed at her bottom lip. Mr. Jackdaw took a sip of his tea and placed it back in its saucer with a little clinking sound that got the Valkyrie's attention. Then he cleared his throat.

"Madam, this is a mission of the utmost importance to king and country. This is no simple errand, and of all the agents I could have approached, I have chosen you. Now, we both know what you expected when you heard I was from the Yard. You don't want to be the Valkyrie anymore because the Valkyrie did some terrible things for terrible people. Well, madam, the past does not just disappear into the ether. Miss Troughton does not get to erase the Valkyrie and all she has done. But perhaps she can find redemption— even use her strength for good. Perhaps you can do something for the Yard, and the Yard can take that into account when considering everything that has happened in the past. And in the end, perhaps the Valkyrie can cease being a terrible shadow in your past and become instead a shining light at the very center of your life. Something beautiful."

Mr. Jackdaw's little speech had swerved between flattery, patriotism, and veiled threats so quickly it almost terrified me. The Valkyrie was an intelligent woman and would surely recognize this attempt to manipulate her. Which was why I was so surprised when I looked back to her and saw that she was blushing.

"Do you really think I can help?" she said.

"I'm certain of it. There's nobody I'd rather have by my side. But you must be ready to leave at a moment's notice, with everything you might need for a long voyage."

"A long voyage? But I can't leave Ma and Pa. The shop . . ."

"I'll see to all that," said Mr. Jackdaw. "If they need to hire help while you're away, I'll arrange the funds. And when we succeed in this mission, you will be handsomely rewarded. Well enough that you can call your time away from your shop a fine investment. And I promise that you will see some marvelous things too."

"What if we don't succeed?" said the Valkyrie.

"Unthinkable," Mr. Jackdaw said. "But I give my word your family's business will not suffer in any way as a result of this endeavor."

"But what will I tell them?"

Mr. Jackdaw grinned one of his particular grins. "Tell them you've been called to serve your king."

XV
Pirate Stories

The very next day, Mr. Jackdaw appeared again in my school. He was becoming increasingly disheveled, with wrinkles in his jacket and hair sticking up where he had forgotten to flatten it after taking off his hat. One of my classmates had come in with a note to say the headmaster expected me in his office, but Mr. Jackdaw pulled me aside before I could reach the headmaster's door.

"Did the headmaster really want to see me?" I said.

"Oh, yes indeed," Mr. Jackdaw said, in the earnest tone of voice I'd come to recognize as the one he used when he had made up a lie he was proud of. "It turns out you've won a special prize from the king himself for a story you wrote about pirates. You'll be taking part in an event for gifted children in

Penzance. Unfortunately it's all rather hurried. You'll be departing tomorrow."

"Tomorrow? What's actually happening?"

"Your young friend Binns is as brazen as they come. He booked passage on the maiden voyage of that new luxury ocean liner everybody's been talking about. So as a result, I've spent the last who-knows-how-many hours ensuring we will also be on board."

"Blimey," I said. "I've only been on a ferry before. Will it be like that?"

"Well, yes. One could say the RMS *Titanic* is like a ferry—in the same way the Palace of Versailles is like a garden shed. Now, let's go and talk to the headmaster about this pirate story of yours."

Luckily, I knew a thing or two about pirates. Doctor Crispin, headmaster of Judner's School, listened politely as I improvised a story, the one I had supposedly already written. It was about how Blackbeard captured a cabin boy from a merchant vessel. The boy kept escaping, again and again, only to end up on more and more pirate ships. He'd learn something from each captain, then finally meet Blackbeard again, using everything he learned to best Blackbeard in a swordfight and become a hero. Doctor Crispin nodded his turnip-shaped head and said it sounded like a fine thing, and he should like to have a copy, which Mr. Jackdaw said would be a problem on account of a possible anthology that might be made following the event I was going to attend.

"I don't quite follow why this gathering might take a month or more," said Doctor Crispin. "That seems most irregular, and Oliver here already missed a lot of school last year."

"It will form a key part of his education," Mr. Jackdaw said with a grin. At some point he had found the time to flatten down his hair. "He will belong to a group of older children instructing younger children, while at the same time receiving the finest education. The king himself has expressed his approval. There are also arrangements for all students' home tutors to travel with them."

Mr. Jackdaw then presented with a flourish a letter with King George's signature and personal seal on it. As Mr. Jackdaw was currently operating outside the knowledge of Scotland Yard, I had to wonder how he'd gotten it. But Doctor Crispin could hardly argue with the king.

As we took Mr. Jackdaw's motorcar—which he now drove himself, for reasons I didn't enquire into—I asked him if the invitation was a forgery.

"Not so," Mr. Jackdaw said, looking pleased with himself. "The signature is quite real, even if I rewrote what came before it. Now, have you spoken to your dear Mr. Scant?"

"No," I said, "he's been staying away from me. He's doing his valet duties and that's all."

"Then I suppose we just have to go for the . . . *high-impact* approach."

As it transpired, the high-impact approach involved using the same story on Mother that had worked on Doctor Crispin. Her eyes lit up with delight when she saw the old-fashioned scroll from the king. "I knew Ollie was a creative spirit!" she enthused.

She listened intently to all the fabricated details of what I would be doing over the next month "or thereabouts," while Mr. Scant watched from beside the hallway doors. I told Mother how excited I was, that I'd never won this kind of prize before, and that I was sure I could make new friends. She hugged me and said she wished I wouldn't keep going off on these "adventures"—which made me look at her suspiciously—but that this sounded too important to turn down.

Of course, the difficult part was talking to Mr. Scant after Mr. Jackdaw had left. We met in the music room, the place we had first spoken openly about his secret life as a thief. To my surprise, he seemed apologetic.

"You know I don't trust Jackdaw," he said. "Even if he appears to be acting out of desperation, I feel certain this was all calculated well in advance. I wouldn't be surprised if he knew we would have the diamond stolen from us. But still, I take it you have made your mind up to go with him?"

I nodded. "I think we have to do all we can to stop Aurelian. And I can see life getting a lot more complicated if we don't get that diamond."

"Maybe it belongs back where it came from," said Mr. Scant. "Maybe it should be in this new unified South Africa. That's what I was known for, wasn't it? Returning things to where they came from."

"When they were stolen," I said. "Not things that have been properly bought and sold."

"I wish I could be certain that's what happened with that diamond."

"What matters is that Aurelian will sell it for money that he'll use to do terrible things. Do you think *he's* the rightful owner? If he's not, you should do what you've always done: steal from a thief."

With that, Mr. Scant stepped forward until he

was bearing down on me. "I know what should be done. I know what *should have* been done. But I don't know if I'm capable of doing it. With Hunter there, I don't know that I can do anything at all."

"I don't know why it matters to you so much," I said. "Don't you want to talk to him, and find out why he's here, why he's working with Aurelian?"

"It's not something I can explain in words," said Mr. Scant. "The point is that you can't rely on me to protect you this time. I can't rely on myself—for anything."

"I've learned a lot from you, Mr. Scant," I said. "I'll go alone if I have to, but I'd feel a lot better if you were there. And if it comes to fighting, it's okay. I've got help."

"Help?" Mr. Scant thought for a moment. "Mykolas's fighting days are over after that bullet wound. Who else is there?"

"We . . . asked the Valkyrie."

"The *Valkyrie*? Have you forgotten she worked for the Society for most of her life?"

"That's the past. We're giving her a chance to move on. Maybe that's what you need to do too."

Mr. Scant gave me a long, steady look and then nodded.

"You're the best," I said, preparing to clap him on the shoulder but thinking better of it.

Father was the last person to convince. He knew at once that my trip would involve something more serious than the reciting of a pirate story, but he mumbled his approval and said, "I suppose you'd better take Scant with you again. He's good at these things. And, sad to say, I don't have much use for him just now, being in the office all day to deal with this wretched coal strike."

"Thank you, Father," I said, giving him a hug that seemed to quite startle him.

And so it was that on Wednesday, 10th April, Mr. Jackdaw met us at the crack of dawn and took us to Southampton. We entered first a little police station near the docks where he knew the officers on duty. He showed us into a room for a briefing, and there, waiting for us with a shy look on her face, was the Valkyrie.

"Gosh!" I said, a response that seemed to disappoint her. An attempt had been made to dress her in fine travelling clothes, with an elegant dress, pearls, and a fancy hat with flowers. "Oh, I'm sorry," I added hastily. "I didn't recognize you at first. You look very fine, I'm just used to seeing you in the apron and . . . breastplate."

"I know I look a sight," she said. "Don't rub it in."

"A sight? A vision," said Mr. Jackdaw. "And that brings me to the matter at hand. We're about to travel under assumed names, for which I've made arrangements. Here are your passports. Matilda and I are Mr. and Mrs. Booth, a surgeon and his wife." For a moment, he looked a little flushed with pleasure at the thought of it. "The two of you are Jacob and Aaron Fisher, father and son. Jacob, you are a fashionable London hatmaker."

He gave each of us our travel documents and tickets, which looked as fine as wedding invitations. "First class?" I said. "That must be why we're getting all dressed up."

"Indeed," said Mr. Jackdaw. "Thankfully only half the tickets for this voyage had sold, so with some backs scratched and strings pulled, I got us abroad at a low cost. But do take care not to draw too much attention. I would have put you two in steerage, but then you wouldn't be able to come up to the first-class decks."

"Why not?" I asked.

"American immigration law," said Mr. Jackdaw. "Everyone in steerage is going for a new life in America. They get off at a different port from the other tourists. Immigration procedures, you see. If the people in steerage could come to the second-class decks, they could simply slip away into the streets of New York upon disembarking."

"America?" said Mr. Scant. "I thought we were bound for the Cape."

"A little strange, I must confess," said Mr. Jackdaw. "From what I gather, this voyage will be where the Binns boy makes the sale. I think the grandiosity of this liner appeals to young Aurelian's sense of drama. The buyer will then take the diamond to South Africa on a different ship."

"How are we sure this isn't a red herring?" said Mr. Scant. "That Binns didn't leave this trail for us so we get on the boat while he's somewhere else altogether?"

"I considered it. We're going to confirm the boy is on board before we depart. But from the brazenness of it all, I feel as though Binns's message is that he doesn't care if we know his plans or not."

"I have a question," said the Valkyrie.

"Yes?"

"If we're husband and wife, are we to . . . share quarters?"

"Ah, not to worry. The room will have a partition, so you have nothing to fear!"

The Valkyrie didn't look entirely convinced by that.

"The departure time is noon," said Mr. Scant. "We don't have time to dawdle."

"We are still on schedule," said Mr. Jackdaw. "Let's change into the clothes befitting surgeons and premier hatmakers. Then we can go and see for ourselves this ship they call unsinkable."

XVI
First Class

Docks and shipyards dominated Southampton, with a number of vessels floating like immense seabirds around wharfs where the city met the sea. Great crowds had gathered to see the maiden voyage of this brand new Olympic-class ocean liner, but most of them were on the promenade below our walkway.

After porters took our belongings and ship's officers inspected our documents, we approached the *Titanic*. I paused before boarding and marveled. As high as we were on the elevated walkway between the pier and the ship, the *Titanic* stood far taller still. Her sheer size was almost terrifying, with four vast smokestacks stretching up into the sky like the fingers of some ancient god. Or perhaps like a titan.

The portholes farthest from me were little more

than pin-pricks, but each one represented a cabin. Even only half full, the ship would have thousands of people on board. How would we possibly find Aurelian?

A portly man with walrus moustaches cleared his throat loudly behind me, and I realized I was blocking his path. Nodding to him apologetically, I made my way inside.

We stood next at the top of a staircase more grandiose than the one at my home. It swept down to a lower deck, with its dark wood shining in the natural daylight that poured in from a great glass dome that would have suited a cathedral. A white-bearded, jovial man came to shake our hands and welcomed us aboard, introducing himself as Captain Smith. When Mr. Jackdaw gave our assumed names, the captain's expression changed just for a moment, but he said, "Welcome aboard. Please enjoy the finest ship the world has ever seen."

Captain Smith had hundreds of passengers to greet, so we moved on. Still, I chanced a look back at him, trying to determine whether or not Mr. Jackdaw had told him we weren't who we claimed to be.

A smiling steward who had listened out for our names showed us down the sweeping staircase. When we reached our rooms, I couldn't see the one Mr. Jackdaw would be sharing with the Valkyrie, but the one meant for Jacob and Aaron Fisher, the hatmaker and his son, was very fine. It had dark, wooden-paneled walls and two small but comfortable-looking beds on either side of a little round table. Dark green accents on the room's upholstery matched well with the patterned carpet.

After only a few moments, a knock came at the door. I turned the handle to see the Valkyrie. She looked rather troubled, but Mr. Jackdaw was smiling behind her.

"Your room looks nice," she said. "Ours is a little small, but thank goodness we can divide it in two. I'd rather we get this business over and done with quickly."

We decided to go to the first-class lounge, back up near the top of the ship. It was a cavern of a place, with a grand fireplace at the center and a huge chandelier above it. Dozens of comfortable-looking armchairs and sofas were arranged around small tables so that different groups could sit together.

"It's like a palace," I said.

"In the Louis V style," said Mr. Jackdaw. "This is modern luxury. Even your father would have to hesitate before spending the money on extravagance like this."

"I sure he'd say it was a big waste, and we'd go in second class."

"I stick out like a sore thumb," the Valkyrie said. "All these lords and ladies have their noses in the air. I think they get surprised when they can still see someone up here."

"Not *so* many lords and ladies today," Mr. Jackdaw said as we chose some nearby seats. "Baron Pirrie ought to be on board with his nephew, who designed this beauty. Then the Countess of Rothes, and also Baronet Duff-Gordon with his wife."

After a waiter had taken our order for tea, I asked, "Duff-Gordon?" I looked about the room in case I could recognize the famous sportsman. "Maybe I can ask him about my fencing."

"Well, perhaps," said Mr. Jackdaw. "But don't draw attention to yourself. You'll stand out enough being one of the only children in first class. And do remember that first and foremost, we're on the lookout for Binns and his contact."

"Do we know who his contact is?"

"No," Mr. Jackdaw said. "There's a family from South Africa in second class and some other South

African passengers in third class, but having researched them all, I very much doubt he'll be meeting them."

"What about Hunter?" said Mr. Scant, avoiding meeting Mr. Jackdaw's eye by pouring the tea. "Will he be on board?"

"I think not," said Mr. Jackdaw. "It's possible he's using another name, just as we are. But, well . . . if children stand out, it's nowhere near as much as he would."

"How do you mean?" I said. "What about the South African family?"

"A white family."

"Ah," I said, realizing what he meant by "standing out."

"That said, there are in fact a number of international passengers on board," Mr. Jackdaw said. "In second class, a fellow from Japan. A cabin full of Chinese folk are in third class, off for a new life in the New World, I suppose, though they'll have to contend with that beastly Exclusion Act. Two fellows of Egyptian descent will also join us in first class once we get to France."

"I wish I knew what to look for," the Valkyrie said. "I'm not even sure I'd recognize Aurelian Binns after three years."

"He's taller than his father now," Mr. Scant said. "Almost my height."

"He never did take after either of his parents," the Valkyrie said. "Except for that mean streak of theirs."

After finishing our tea, we set about looking for Aurelian. There was no sign of him in any of the public areas, from the smoking room to the prom-enade deck, where the great majority of passengers had gathered to wave to people at the pier. As we prepared to depart, people called to loved ones and waved kerchiefs in the air. I couldn't find a lot of space between them, but I squeezed myself into a spot between a squat older lady in a large hat and a suave young man who smelled of cigarettes. I looked in wonderment at the mass of people waving off the ship. After a few moments, though, the crowd around me pressed closer, and feeling crushed, I withdrew.

Mr. Scant and Mr. Jackdaw continued scanning the crowd, while the Valkyrie steadied herself against a post, looking queasy.

"Any sign of Aurelian?" I said, but they shook their heads. "Maybe we should ask if anyone has seen him."

"Ask whoever you can," said Mr. Jackdaw, "but there's a time and place for conversation, and I don't think most of this lot will be interested in it just now. We ought to wait until we're sharing luncheon or brandies."

I nodded, glancing about but seeing only people's backs or small groups of passengers talking amongst themselves. Then I noticed two children a little further down the deck. A boy and a girl, presumably siblings, with one of those funny dogs with a rectangular head and a little beard. The girl must have been about my age, her brother a few years younger. A maid was standing quietly by, keeping an eye on them. I decided to speak with the pair.

"I like your dog," I said. "Can I say hello?"

The boy looked at me, then to his sister, who said in a clear, confident American accent, "He's called Brinny. I'm called Lucile, and this is William. Say hello, William."

"Hello there," said the boy. "Go ahead, he's a good dog."

So I knelt and stroked the handsome brown dog and introduced myself. "I'm O—uh, Jacob," I said, then quickly added, "This is my first time on a ship this size."

Brinny the dog regarded me with curiosity, but it was hard to tell if he appreciated the attention or not.

"Isn't it gargantuan?" Lucile said in the tone of someone very proud of her vocabulary. "But it takes such a long time to go across the ocean. We live in Europe now but we go to New York every year. At first it's fun, but after three or four days, oh, it's interminable."

"I suppose it takes a long time," I said.

"It's *interminable*!" said Lucile.

"I once went all the way to China in an airship," I told the pair. "It wasn't very luxurious, though."

"I'm sure Father could pay someone to make it more luxurious. I should ask him."

"Say, have you ever been in a motorcar?" William said excitedly.

"Oh yes, many times," I said. "My father loves motorcars."

"Oh." William looked a little disappointed.

I then remembered that I was supposed to be Jacob Fisher, so I lamely added, "Almost as much as he loves hats."

"I'm sure he'd love to try Papa's brand new motorcar," said Lucile. "It's in the cargo hold. It's quite the thing!"

"I'm sure he would," I said, smiling.

"We're going to have a ride when we get back

home," William said. "I'm going to learn to drive it."

"Lucky you. Oh, I'm looking for a relative of mine, but I haven't found him yet. Maybe you've seen him? He's older than me, seventeen or eighteen. He likes wearing nice clothes—erm . . ."

"Whole lot of people like that here," Lucile said, gesturing to the assembled crowd.

"Well, one thing, he has long hair," I told her. "Like one of the musketeers, I suppose. Perhaps not that long, but longer than anybody's I can see here. Have you seen someone like that?"

The two children shook their heads. I was about to say something else, but I saw Mr. Scant and Mr. Jackdaw coming toward me. I went over to my mentor while Mr. Jackdaw shined his teeth at the siblings and their maid. "Terribly sorry, but the boy's mother is calling for him. He went off on his own, you see, and with these crowds, well, best to fetch him, what? Don't want to put an oar in their boat or rock the boat when on such a boat as this! Just want to make sure we're all on the same boat."

"Why did you do that?" I said, as Mr. Jackdaw and Mr. Scant ushered me away. "They might have seen something useful."

"Some old priest's coming this way taking

pictures of everything," said Mr. Jackdaw. "The last thing we want to happen is to get photographed."

Finding the Valkyrie after that was a simple matter. She was always the tallest person in the vicinity, especially in her big fashionable hat. "They say we're about to launch," she said. "Master Diplexito, would you like to sit on my shoulders to watch?"

I almost laughed. "Firstly, no thank you, I'm a bit old for that. Secondly, I'm Jacob Fisher here, remember?"

"Ah, sorry," she said, rubbing her temple as though it were all a bit too much to remember.

"Thirdly, once this is all over and done with, please call me Ollie. We're friends now."

"Friends?"

"We're all friends here," Mr. Jackdaw said, moving to take the Valkyrie's hand for a gentlemanly kiss. A ship-wide shudder gave her a chance to stumble away.

"Ah! It must be noon," she said. "We're casting off."

The voices of the people calling to their loved ones swelled louder, passengers on the steerage decks below filling the air with cheerful whoops and whistles.

"Keep watching for Binns," Mr. Scant said, but we stayed where we were as the vast floating monolith beneath us set in motion. Through a trembling under my feet, I could feel the immense power of the engines, and somewhere a great whistle sounded.

After a few minutes, people had started to relax and move away from the rails of the promenade deck. But around that same time, that the air changed. I began to hear concerned voices from further aft. "Something's wrong," I said.

It wasn't immediately clear what was happening— the crowd around us was still thick enough to keep us from rushing to the railings. But we began to understand. Another nearby ship, almost as large as ours, was moving very strangely. Its stern was swinging out from where it had been moored. And in a few more minutes, we were going to hit it.

XVII
Jewels and Grime

eep your eyes open," said Mr. Scant. "This is exactly the sort of irregularity we don't need."

A crowd had gathered to watch the crisis unfold, which made it hard for me to see. With such enormous ships, everything happened very slowly, but a grim sense of inevitability about a collision overtook the crowd. The rumbling beneath our feet got stronger, and it became clear our captain was bringing our ship about. Someone said a tugboat was going to pull the other ship away, but it kept coming closer and closer.

"If it gets much nearer, we'll hit," said Mr. Jackdaw.

"Or somebody could jump from this ship to the next," said Mr. Scant. "Watch carefully."

The other ship came so close that I gripped a handrail so I wouldn't be thrown from my feet by the impact. But to everyone's relief, the two liners missed one another by what looked like barely enough space in which to drop a billiard ball. Mr. Scant's suspicions were likewise unfounded. Nobody jumped from vessel to vessel, which everybody would have been able to see in any case. Soon we were satisfied that the disaster was averted, and when my stomach growled, we decided to go to the dining room for lunch.

The drama hadn't prevented the kitchen staff from preparing a buffet, so I piled as much roast beef as I thought I could get away with on my plate.

"This is the life!" I declared.

"You can say that again," said the Valkyrie, who had opted for a veal pie with daintily sliced vegetables. "The meat is remarkably high-quality. I wonder how they're storing it."

"Let's stay alert now," Mr. Jackdaw said, scanning the room. "We're not here to muck about."

"I haven't seen the Binns boy anywhere," said Mr. Scant. "Even amidst this many people, he'd be easy to spot."

"He must be on board," said Mr. Jackdaw. "A steward said he was, but he also told me Aurelian's moved cabins. In any case, catching him won't be a matter of knocking on his door. If he doesn't want to be found, it wouldn't be difficult to hide."

"For an evening, perhaps, but not for day after day," said Mr. Scant. "After we eat, we search."

"What about the other boat?" I said. "Could he have been behind that?"

"I wouldn't think so," said Mr. Jackdaw. "A collision on that scale would be a very difficult thing to arrange, and for what? He makes another boat hit this one—what advantage does that give him? No, I think we can chalk that one up to bad luck."

"So how are we going to search?" I asked. "All together?"

"Splitting up would be wiser," said Mr. Jackdaw. "But for safety's sake, not one by one. Two by two makes the most sense, no?"

"Yes, but perhaps not the way you're thinking," said Mr. Scant. "I still don't trust myself. You and I can look after ourselves, Jackdaw, but I don't want to put Master Oliver in any more danger than he needs to be. I think Miss Troughton ought to go with the boy." He turned to me. "And after all, you're friends now, are you not?"

And so it was that I began to explore the ship

with the Valkyrie. I had grown a fair bit since the first time I met her, in an abandoned underground resort where she was trying to kill me. But Matilda Troughton still stood about twice as tall as I did and boasted far more muscle. It was strange seeing her in a fashionable dress, and I wondered where Mr. Jackdaw had gotten hold of it so soon. Sometimes we heard laughter behind us, especially from the young men on board, which may or may not have followed some cruel comment. But for her part, she nodded graciously to anyone who caught her eye and returned any polite greetings.

"Mr. Jackdaw seems to have taken a liking to you," I said.

"Do you think so?" said the Valkyrie. "I never know if anything he says is true."

"Well, I can understand that."

"I think he's just saying things to keep me off my guard," said the Valkyrie. "He probably thinks I'll be easier to deal with that way."

"I hadn't thought of that."

We made our way around the public facilities of the ship, which were extensive and as fine as those of any country club. The F deck held a Turkish bath, which sounded like a good place to hide, but the attendant said nobody was inside. Outside a gymnasium, we met another two children, an older sister and a younger brother, whose mouths fell open as they saw the Valkyrie. They were younger than the other brother and sister I had met and told us in Scottish accents that they hadn't seen anybody like Aurelian. The pair was only travelling as far as France and getting off there.

"I forgot about people getting on and off at the other ports," I said. "Maybe Aurelian's buyer isn't on board yet, and Aurelian's hiding until they arrive."

After more than two hours of searching, we came across what we thought was the grand staircase we had seen when we first boarded. "We can go back to the lounge from here," said the Valkyrie.

"Hold on," I said. "I think this is a different staircase. Look at the clock. The one we saw before had all that fancy carving around it. This one is only small."

"How many can there be?" the Valkyrie said, and then we heard laughter from above. The Valkyrie flushed and pulled her hat down to hide her face.

"Oh, do pardon us," an older woman said, coming down the steps to apologize. "We only laughed because we said the very same thing earlier. How do you do? My name is Mary Fortune. These are my daughters, Ethel, Alice, and Mabel."

The daughters, all grown women, slim and elegant, gave little curtseys.

"My name is Booth. Erm . . . *Mildred* Booth," the Valkyrie said. Mr. Jackdaw had obviously never told her what her forename was meant to be. "This is the son of my husband's dear friend. His name is Jacob."

"Pleased to meet you," I said. "Are none of you married?"

"Why! What a forward question," the oldest, Ethel, said.

"Oh, it's only that if you're not, you'd be Miss Fortune, Miss Fortune and Miss Fortune." I smiled. "That seems a touch unlucky."

The four women laughed. "As it happens, we are not married," Miss Mabel Fortune said.

"And you don't know the half of it," Miss Alice Fortune said with a cheeky smile. "When I was in Cairo, a fortune-teller told me I will lose everything but my life by travelling on the sea. 'Oh, great danger,' he said. We Miss Fortunes must be a cursed and sorry lot!"

"Oh, I don't think I like the sound of that," said the Valkyrie. "You gave me a shiver."

The mother looked amused. "What a fine tall lady you are, Mrs. Booth. And Master Jacob, I can tell you're a clever one. You must join us at our dinner table tonight."

"We'd be honored," the Valkyrie said. "I've never had friends from America before."

"And you still haven't," Mrs. Fortune said in playful reproach. "We are Canadians."

The search continued for the rest of the day, though we often stopped to enjoy the *Titanic*'s many luxuries, riding in the elevator for the novelty of it and visiting the promenade deck to enjoy the fresh air. The Valkyrie and I even went to the second-class facilities, where signage suggested we'd find a library. It was little more than a writing room, in truth, where a number of passengers were writing letters to send home. Throughout the experience, we encountered no sign of Aurelian Binns, but the more we saw, the more we realized just how many places there were to hide.

The ship dropped anchor at France that evening, while my party gathered for dinner with the Fortunes. Mrs. Fortune repeated my little joke to her husband, who rolled his eyes. "We've heard that one a few times," he said, but laughed all the same.

Mr. Jackdaw stoked the engines of his distinctive charm, asking all sorts of questions about Mr. Fortune's property business. I had to try not to laugh when the Fortunes asked Mr. Scant about his hat-making secret and he said, "Well, you know, it's, er . . . best not to do anything too outrageous. Just stay close to the trends and put a small unique spin to it so that you stand out."

After dinner, a number of new passengers had arrived. Groups moved about first class, meeting one another and reaffirming old friendships, but of Aurelian there was no sign. I thought I spotted him for a moment, behind a loud American lady who kept throwing her head back to guffaw. But when I darted around her, I could see no trace of him. In the end, we retired for the night, promising tomorrow we would search every inch of the liner if we had to.

With the constant movement of the ship, I found it hard to sleep. And so as I lay in my small bed, I imagined some of the remarkable things I'd overhead about the ship. Her rudder weighed more than a hundred tons and needed special engines to move it. And almost two hundred men worked night and day to feed coal into the great engines. But my mattress was so comfortable and the fine dining so heavy in my stomach that before long, I was drifting off after all.

Mr. Scant woke me at seven the next morning and left me to dress myself. I decided on my warmest gray waistcoat and jacket, the ones Mother had ordered from an expensive catalogue. The other children and teenagers had worn similar clothes yesterday, so I was sure nobody would think I looked out of place. We met Mr. Jackdaw and the Valkyrie at breakfast, both of them dressed up again in fine but somewhat more comfortable-looking clothes. The Valkyrie seemed very tired and said she could never sleep well in a room that wasn't her own.

"How did you sleep, my boy?" asked Mr. Jackdaw.

"Surprisingly well," I said.

"Mr. Scant wasn't snoring too much?"

"I sleep in silence," said Mr. Scant.

The *Titanic* was due to stop at one more city before crossing the Atlantic Ocean—Queenstown, Ireland, this time. After that, we would begin the voyage to America at about lunchtime.

"We have to keep searching," said Mr. Jackdaw.

And so search we did. As the Valkyrie walked around the promenade deck for the third time, she decided to strike up a conversation with me.

"I'm thinking of becoming a suffragette," she said.

I wasn't sure how to respond for a moment. "One of those ladies who chain themselves up to railings?"

"For the sake of getting *votes*, yes."

"Father says it's a lot of silly nonsense."

The Valkyrie paused. "So what do *you* think?"

"I'm not sure I know enough about it."

"Oh? Well, what's your first impression?"

"Well, we do say Queen Victoria was the best monarch we ever had, but even *she* wouldn't have been able to vote. I think that's a bit strange. And, you know, why should Jack the Ripper's view count more than Miss Florence Nightingale's? I can't say I really understand politics."

"I think you understand better than a lot of people I know," said the Valkyrie. "I spoke to that Mr. Jackdaw about it, and he said intelligence doesn't come into it. Women have motherly instincts, he told me, and want to care for the poorest and most vulnerable. He thinks we'd be fooled into squandering all the wealth of the Empire—letting the poor take it all and spend it on having more children. Such a narrow view. And the worst part was that he said it so nicely. Like he assumed I wouldn't understand that what he was saying was selfish."

"Mr. Scant always said you were a very clever person."

"He did? Oh, when I remember those days, running about with my cleavers and squeezing money out of business owners. I don't feel like I was in the least bit clever. I was a fool."

"But good at fighting," I said, leaning down over the rail. "And wiser now." Ahead of us, the vessel's pointed bow reached forward like the axe-head of some god of war.

"It seems to me nothing's about to change in England without a fight," said the Valkyrie. "So maybe fighting would be some help to these suffragettes. My only worry is that if I join them and then it all comes out, everything I did in the past, well, that might be a bad thing for the movement. I don't know if I could live with the shame."

"Some of them get taken off to prison already, don't they?" I said. "I don't suppose they'd be that troubled."

"Ah, but it's a big difference, isn't it? They're going to prison for their cause. I deserve to be put in prison for other things altogether."

"I suppose," I said, putting my chin down on the rail. We'd seen the view below several times before.

There was seating for the steerage passengers, but they must have been divided by sex, because I could spot only men. The weather was cold at the moment, so there weren't many on the deck, but a few sat there enjoying themselves with card games or newspapers. I looked past them to the forecastle, a raised area near the front of the ship where all manner of cranes and tools could be found, as well as the ship's anchor— apparently the biggest and heaviest ever made. I felt a little sad that passengers were forbidden from going out to see it. Which was when I noticed a figure there.

I stood up straight, then leaned forward, squinting to make sure I had really seen what I thought I had seen.

"What is it?" asked the Valkyrie.

"There's someone up on the forecastle."

"Those sailors?"

"No," I said, "past them. Right up at the end. I think it's him—his outline's different from the rest. I think it's Aurelian."

"What's would he be doing there?"

"He's not doing anything. He's just . . . standing."

"We should get the others."

"What?" I said. "No, we'll lose him. We need to get down there."

"Why don't you go and find Mr. Scant, and I'll keep an eye on him."

"It's all men below. I'm sure they'll kick up a big fuss if you're down there. I'm going. You find Mr. Scant and Mr. Jackdaw."

"I don't think I should leave you alone."

"If I've learnt one thing from Mr. Scant," I said, "it's been following people without them seeing me."

The Valkyrie hesitated for a moment but then nodded and withdrew. I couldn't reach the forecastle without going lower first. So I ran down the steps that led to B deck. It was level with forecastle, but I couldn't get there without first going down again and crossing the well deck. At the bottom of the next flight of stairs, a little gate stood to remind the steerage passengers not to come up into the first class area. Nobody seemed to care that I went through it the opposite way, dashing out amongst the steerage passengers. I had to dart through the men gathered there as best as I could, which most of them seemed to find amusing.

"Steady on, lad!"

"Sorry, pardon me."

"Bloody 'ell, what's the rush?"

"Just got to get through, excuse me."

"Now what in tarnation?"

"I do beg your pardon."

So it went until I reached the steep steps leading up to the forecastle. That's when more people took notice, as a nearby sign clearly said no passengers should go beyond that point. I rushed up undeterred and made for the breakwater, a big barrier that directed water across the forecastle and away from the well deck below. Some sailors were there, at the base of the big mast for the telegraph wires, and they came at once to stop me.

"Oi, you there!" called a red-faced seaman with a nose like a cauliflower. "You can't be here. No passengers!"

I ignored him and vaulted over the breakwater and onto the deck beyond. I found all manner of chains and cranks there, but no sign of Aurelian. Certain by now that I had seen him, I peered around the enormous anchor at the prow of the ship, but by then the sailors were trying to surround me.

"It's dangerous, boyo," another sailor said, a man with a bushy ginger beard. "Come back here where it's safe."

Then a clear voice sounded from the first-class deck. Not a shout, but it carried over the rest, as if the speaker were trained for the theater. I recognized it at once. Aurelian.

"Don't hurt him!" he cried out. "He's my brother and he's only doing it for a dare. It's all right, William! You win! You won the bet. Just come back now."

I glared at him and started back toward the steps. The big-nosed sailor grabbed my arm and pushed me toward the breakwater when I was close enough. "It's bloody dangerous here," he growled. "One big wave and we're all swept overboard. No place for games."

"I'm sorry," I said as I climbed. "He dared me."

"Bloody idiot. If you weren't some little lord, I'd give you such a smack."

The passengers all seemed very amused by me as I made my way back through them. Some applauded, others jeered. One asked me to stay around and have a cigarette, which I politely declined. As I reached the stairs to the first-class section, the rough seaman gave one last barb. "Go on, back where you belong, up with the toffs."

By then I didn't care what the man thought of me. I had only one thing on my mind, and that was finding Aurelian. He wasn't waiting for me when I reached the place he had shouted from, but I could see him walking away down the promenade—slowly enough that he must have known I'd spot him.

Each time I turned a new corner, Aurelian rounded the next one. I knew he was leading me in a game of cat and mouse, but I could do nothing except play along. He led me down another flight of steps, into the second-class area, and back out onto another deck. I kept hoping I would run into Mr. Scant or the Valkyrie, but they were nowhere to be seen. Down another flight of steps we went, and then I saw Aurelian disappear through a doorway. A sign clearly read, *No passengers beyond this point*, but that was where Aurelian had gone.

I took out my pocket handkerchief and stepped inside, closing the door behind me in such a way that the handkerchief would be caught in the doorway. Now if the others came along, they'd see where I had gone.

Despite the polished beauty of the *Titanic*'s passenger areas, its bowels were plain and already grimy, even on the ship's maiden voyage. I supposed they had been grimy from the day they were made. The walkways and staircases were made of iron, not polished wood. Huge pipes ran this way and that, and strange valves and gauges lined the walls.

I heard Aurelian before I saw him again.

"Playing the hero, Master Oliver?"

"Where are you?" I said.

"Why? If you caught me, what would you do, all alone?"

"I'd do whatever I could to stop you," I said.

He laughed, and I tried to follow the sound. He was most certainly below me, so I started down the closest flight of iron steps.

"You know, I envy you," he said. "That simple view of the world. That lack of understanding."

"That doesn't sound like envy," I said to the darkness.

"But it is. To be so unaware of this world's true face . . . To believe yourself a force for good as you do nothing but take from others . . ."

The only way down from where I stood was a ladder, at least ten feet tall from the look of it. I eased myself onto it, working to keep Aurelian talking, to keep leading me to him.

"That's rich!" I said. "The one who steals a diamond says I take from others."

Suddenly he was above me, his narrow face twisted in fury. He reached down and grabbed my wrists, pulling them away from the ladder.

"*You have no idea what you've taken from me!*" he snarled, and then he let me drop.

I had no way to stop myself falling. For a moment I thought I could somehow catch myself on the ladder, but I landed hard on the solid metal walkway below. The back of my head hit the surface hard, and my vision swam. For a terrifying moment, I couldn't tell which way was up or down. Aurelian stood over me, enjoying my helplessness.

"You took my family from me. You took my father. My mother too. Tore my family legacy to pieces. But you don't know anything about your mentor or what he is to *me*. You still think your dear Mr. Scant and his idiot of a brother just accidentally stumbled upon hidden societies?"

As I managed to gasp my first breath since I fell, Aurelian wrapped a hand around my neck and pulled me to my feet, his long hair hanging about his face like a willow tree at midnight.

"Slowly, Oliver Diplexito, I'm going to watch as you come to understand. I want to be there when your world crumbles. And I want you to know that I made it happen."

Even though I wanted to fight him, even though I tried to stand, my legs failed me, and I crumpled down at his feet. Little fireworks flashed in front of my eyes. When my vision cleared, Aurelian was staring upwards.

"Ah. Here they come," he said, then stepped over me and began to run back the way I had chased him. I twisted to watch him sprint down a passageway until he nearly disappeared. A few moments later, Mr. Scant landed beside me. In the dim light, his golden claw seemed to gleam.

"He went that way," I managed to croak.

"Are you hurt?"

"No. Just fell. He dropped me."

"This way!" he called upward. Above me, I could hear Mr. Jackdaw and the Valkyrie following.

"I'm coming too," I said, getting up onto my knees.

"Can you manage?"

"I'll do my best."

Aurelian was still toying with us, laughing as he stayed just in sight.

"He's leading us into a trap," said the Valkyrie.

"No doubt," said Mr. Scant. "We'd better catch him before we get there."

But Aurelian knew where he was going and stayed too far ahead to catch. I struggled to keep up until I was no longer pursuing Aurelian but rather pursuing Mr. Jackdaw, the last of my three companions I could see. Once or twice we passed strangers—men with faces completely covered with soot, or rough-looking fellows with flat caps and stubble—but they only watched us pass with mouths agape.

Finally, I caught up to the others at a hatch that the Valkyrie must have struggled to fit through. Inside was a series of ladders and steep staircases, going both upwards and further down. I had imagined we had already been at the very bottom of the ship, but evidently the vessel went even deeper. Far above us was a half-circle of daylight.

"Where are we?" I said.

"I think this is one of the funnels," said Mr. Scant. "But I see no exhaust coming up."

"The fourth stack is a dummy," said Mr. Jackdaw. "A bit of kitchen steam and ventilation. They have it to make the ship look big and important, you see. We must be inside."

"There's Aurelian!" I said. He was above us and climbing fast.

"He'll have nowhere to go," said Mr. Jackdaw. "We can corner him here."

"I wonder," Mr. Scant said.

"Come on," I urged the others. "We can catch him and put a stop to all this!"

We began to climb. Despite Aurelian's youth, he was not as fast as Mr. Scant, and the distance between the two of them soon diminished. I was doing my best, but I once again found myself trailing behind. This time I wasn't alone. Although the Valkyrie showed no sign of tiring out, she wasn't able to scale the ladders as fast as Mr. Scant could, while Mr. Jackdaw was hampered by the bullet wound on his thigh.

"Give it up! We've got you!" she shouted. "Hand over the diamond or you'll get what's coming to you."

Aurelian's laugh seemed to echo all around us. "Why on Earth would I risk bringing the diamond onto a ship like this?" he called down.

I stopped climbing.

"Don't be ridiculous," Aurelian went on. "My associate Mr. Hunter has the diamond. He left from Gravesend for Cape Town this morning."

"Don't believe him!" I said. "We can still arrest him for stealing it."

"Really now?" Aurelian said—and jumped. Not upwards but outwards, into the center of the funnel. For a moment, I thought he had lost his mind, but there was a cable of some sort in his hand, and in moments he was sliding down past us. My eye caught his as he dropped below, and I could see the smirk on his face.

"Two can play at that game," Mr. Scant said, vaulting over the handrail. One of the talons of his claw sprang loose and wound around the metal rails, slowing his descent.

"Too slow," Aurelian said, landing on a lower platform and dashing for the same hatch we had come in through. "This door seals from outside. And I do believe we've arrived at Queenstown, my port of call. *Adieu!*"

Before Mr. Scant could catch him, the hatch closed, followed by a grinding sound that must have been a lock sliding into place. I heard Mr. Scant's feet land on metal, a sound I wasn't used to hearing— evidently he had decided there was no need for stealth. And then we were all alone in the tall, dark dummy funnel of the world's grandest ocean liner.

XVIII
The Napier V

Mr. Scant pounded at the hatch for a little while, then tried to find some gap or slat he could slip the blades of his claw into, but we all knew it was hopeless.

"Are we trapped in here?" I asked.

"Not trapped," said Mr. Scant. "Look up, you can see the sky. We're assured of a way out. But we need a quicker one."

"What's the point?" said a glum Mr. Jackdaw. "The diamond isn't even on board."

"Only if you believe Aurelian," I said. "And even if that were the truth, we know he's going to Cape Town to make the sale. We can still stop him."

"Everything he did was timed with precision," said Mr. Scant. "We're in here because he knows for certain there's no way we can escape in time to stop him getting off this boat."

"Mr. Scant, can you use your claw to pull us to the top?" I asked.

"The motor's built to bring the claw back in," said Mr. Scant. "Not to pull four people up fifty feet. We could use the cable to climb, but it would take just as long as the ladders and be more dangerous besides. Once we reach the top, it will help us get us down to the deck from the outside, though."

"Beg pardon?" said the Valkyrie. "You can't mean we're going to climb down the *outside* of this thing? I'm not much of a climber."

"By all means search for another way out," said Mr. Scant.

"No!" I said. "We need to stay together, otherwise we won't be able to chase Aurelian. Miss Troughton, you're the Valkyrie. A little thing like this can't hold you back."

The Valkyrie drew herself up to her full impressive height. "I'll do what I can."

And so we began our climb up what seemed like an endless number of ladders linked by metal walkways. I started to get tired about four stories up but shook my head every time the adults asked if I needed help.

When we reached the very top of the funnel, we saw that half of it was capped, but we could exit through two hatches covering the other half. Pushing through them, we came face-to-face with another man covered in soot, looking at us in alarm from where he sat. A smoldering cigarette fell from between his lips.

"Oh, er, hello," I said, breathing heavily after the long climb.

"Who the bloody 'ell are you?" the man asked in a vulgar tone. "You can't be up here."

"Police business, my good man," said Mr. Jackdaw.

The man took him at his word and touched at his hat as a kind of apologetic bow. "Begging your pardon. I won't say nothing . . . here! You can't do that."

He was looking at Mr. Scant now, who peered over the edge of the stack and down to the deck far below. I took the opportunity to do the same.

I found a quite astounding view. The ship's deck was pristine, with lifeboats lined up on either side. I could also see Ireland, though the liner had stopped a long way from the Queenstown dock. Colorful houses covered the city's hills, surrounding its tall, spiky cathedral.

I felt a strange pang of sadness for this unfamiliar place, where today so many would say goodbyes to those they loved, many of those loved ones never to return. Though distant glimpses of the crowds assembled to see this majestic new liner reminded me that as much joy as regret would fill their day.

"Meticulous timing," Mr. Scant said. In the water nearby, the little boat that would ferry departing passengers to Queenstown was drawing away from the *Titanic*—and I could see Aurelian aboard it. We would have no chance to reach him now.

"Let's get on with it," Mr. Scant rumbled. He had affixed the cable from his claw to a rail near the top of the funnel. "It's not long enough to reach all the way down to the deck. So we go first to the pipe directly below us. Then we make our way down that pipe. Ready?"

He didn't wait for an answer, clambering over the funnel's edge. I stretched to watch him and saw he had wrapped the cable around himself. He leaned backward as he lowered himself, using his feet to half-walk, half-bounce down to the thin pipe he had mentioned. Once he made it securely, he called up, "You next, Master Oliver."

And so I took hold of the cable and used it like a climbing rope, heading downward while scraping my feet along the outside of the funnel. The cable was much thinner than a climbing rope, and keeping my grip was a challenge, but soon enough I reached the pipe Mr. Scant had mentioned. It was like a thick drainpipe, and warm to the touch. I pulled at it doubtfully.

"Are you sure this will take our weight?" I asked.

"Not entirely."

I swallowed hard, then continued downwards. Climbing down the pipe proved easier than climbing down the cable. There were various other pipes attached to the outside of the funnel, which I could use as handholds or to stand on for a rest, and finally I dropped to the level of the deck. Once I saw no sailors were coming to accost me, I ducked under the rails and waited for the others.

Mr. Scant called up that Mr. Jackdaw should come next. He and Mr. Scant would support themselves on either side of the pipe, they'd decided, and then they'd help support the Valkyrie as she made her way down. Though she was still wearing her fancy first-class passenger clothes, she moved quickly and confidently down to the pipe. After she got within the reach of Mr. Scant and Mr. Jackdaw, the pair of them steadied her down the rest of the pipe. For her part, she didn't seem too troubled by the climb.

"What do we do now?" I asked once we were all safely on the deck.

"We have to get off this ship," said Mr. Jackdaw. "We can't ride it to America. That's going to take days."

"What can we do? The boat to shore has already left. And we're too far away to swim."

"I'm a strong swimmer," the Valkyrie said. "I can help you get there. There were life vests in our room. I'm certain we can make it."

"No," said Mr. Jackdaw. "It would take too long and be much too dangerous. We need to find the wireless telegraphy room."

"What's that?" I asked.

"Those cables," Mr. Jackdaw said, pointing up to a long wire running the length of the ship, above even the funnels. "They're for the radio room. We can send out a telegraph in Morse code. I say! I say, you! I wonder if you can help me . . ."

He had spotted a seaman and went bounding

over to him. Identifying himself as a Scotland Yard police officer got Mr. Jackdaw shown to the "Marconi Room," up at the other end of the boat deck. From there, Mr. Jackdaw made his transmission.

"To whom did you send a message?" Mr. Scant asked.

"To an old friend of mine named Selwyn. He's sending a man to fetch us."

"Out here?" I said. "Is it a flying machine?"

"Not a flying machine," Mr. Jackdaw. "A motor yacht."

So it was that we left the unsinkable ship. Mr. Scant had run out of cable, so we could no longer be discreet in making our exit. Instead, Mr. Jackdaw again used his authority as a police inspector to get the men on a lower deck to open the same door that departing passengers had used to board the boat. We'd then lower a rope ladder the remaining fifteen or twenty feet to the water.

"How long will it take?" I asked as we waited for the motor yacht. "Perhaps we should go and enjoy the first class facilities a little more before we leave."

"Please stay focused, Master Oliver."

"Just seems a waste, that's all."

We stayed put on the low deck, under the watchful eye of two staff members, even as the great ocean liner shuddered back into motion, beginning to leave Queenstown. After what seemed an hour or more, our motorboat arrived—a very fine but rather small vessel. It sliced through the water as easily as any fish but seemed a little unsteady as it bobbed up and down, matching the speed of the departing *Titanic*.

A slim woman with alert eyes and brown skin pulled off the goggles she had been wearing and smiled. "Long time no see, Agent Featherton."

Mr. Jackdaw nodded respectfully. "Agent Petra."

I wondered if just maybe Featherton was Mr. Jackdaw's real name, as unlikely as that seemed. He turned to us and said, "This is a very dear colleague of mine, Mrs. Petra. She was my senior when I was in training."

"A pleasure to meet you," she said. "Miss Troughton. Mr. Scant. Master Diplexito."

"Nice to meet you too," I said as the others nodded.

"Better come aboard for handshakes," she said, still smiling. "This is Mr. Edge's brand new motorboat, the *Napier V*, designed to set new speed records on the ocean waves."

"She's a beauty," said Mr. Jackdaw.

"Nothing but the best," said Mrs. Petra. "Although you can't bring all those heavy things aboard. Too much weight. Small bags only."

And so we left the famous unsinkable ship—the pinnacle of human scientific achievement and the most luxurious vessel ever opened to the public—by clambering down a rope ladder. I had to leave behind a lot of clothes, but nothing I regretted abandoning. Even without our luggage, however, the little motor yacht was rather a tight fit for all of us.

As we began to speed away on Mrs. Petra's motorboat, I looked back to the ocean liner, the immense floating city. Soon I was able to cover it with a fingertip.

Back on solid ground in Queenstown, Mrs. Petra led us to a nearby café. She ordered a double espresso, which smelled strong enough to make my eyes water.

"What do we do now?" I asked.

"Clearly we have to go on to Cape Town," said Mr. Scant.

"In Africa?" the Valkyrie said. "Nobody mentioned anything about that to me. We've spent all this time running around doing all the wrong things. I have half a mind to just go home."

"Please don't leave us," I said. "We still need you. More than ever."

"I should very much regret seeing you go too," Mr. Jackdaw said, his hand on his heart. "But the diamond is going to Africa, and so must we. That's why I contacted Mrs. Petra. She's our authority on the place."

"*North* Africa," said Mrs. Petra. "Africa is a big continent, and I don't think anybody can be an authority on all of her countries. I was born in Tripoli but I grew up in Cairo, before my father's business and second wife took us to London. And I'm currently spending what's meant to be my home leave acting as support for this rapscallion." She waved a disapproving hand at Mr. Jackdaw, who did his usual grin.

"What was it like growing up in Egypt?" I asked. "I'd like to hear more about it from someone who really lived there."

"You can ask me anything you like later on, when we're on our way," Mrs. Petra said with a smile.

"We're forever indebted to you," said Mr. Jackdaw. "There was nobody else I could turn to."

"Oh, nonsense," she said. "I can think of at least two others who would support you without immediately telling the boss what you're up to. Granted, neither of them are in this hemisphere. And I can't say I fully trust Agent Redwood." She looked directly at me and said, conspiratorially, "He only eats beige-colored food."

"Oh," I said.

"If you have helped us, madam, you have our thanks," said Mr. Scant.

"Less of the 'madam' please," said Mrs. Petra. "I've only found two gray hairs in my head so far, so it's a bit early for that."

Mr. Scant gave a respectful nod.

"Have you found us passage to Cape Town?" Mr. Jackdaw asked Mrs. Petra.

"I have," she said. "I'll take you as far as Plymouth and set you on your way. I can't risk being caught up in your mess any more than I already am."

"I'm grateful you've done as much as you have," said Mr. Jackdaw. "But it's up to us to fix our mistakes. It's our duty to king and country to get that diamond back where it belongs."

"And that's London?" said Mr. Scant.

"Yes. Of course."

"I wanted to be certain," Mr. Scant said, turning away.

"When is the liner from Plymouth?" I asked. "Aurelian has a big head start."

"It leaves the day after tomorrow," said Mrs. Petra. "Noon. A disappointing menu. I checked for you."

"Two days?" I said. "We can't just wait for two days."

"I'm afraid you may not have much of a choice in the matter," said Mrs. Petra. "I'd say you're lucky there's passage from Plymouth at all."

"Thank you for the help, but maybe we can get there faster," I said. "I think Father can help us. Or at least, his business partner. Have any of you met Mr. Beards?"

XIX
Flying Machines

T hese days, Mr. Beards didn't really have much to do.

His business, Binns and Beards Financial Services and Dirigibles, had come to a sad end when Mr. and Mrs. Binns had gone to prison for being the leaders of a criminal cult. But Father had absorbed the airship manufacturing part of their business into his company. Now Mr. Beards pottered about in a supervisory role at one of Father's factories. But his passion for airships remained as strong as ever, which was the important thing for us. We quickly received a reply to our telegraph, with Mr. Beards telling us to wait for him by the Queenstown town hall that very evening.

Mr. Jackdaw had access to a gentleman's club for government employees, so after bidding Mrs. Petra farewell, we waited there discussing what we could have done differently on board the *Titanic*. A few hours later, we approached the town hall with time to spare. The hall was a pretty little building with ornate chimneys and the shape of a brooding hen. It sat on the water's edge, with a little jetty and a length of road nearby. The scene was quiet, and the air was still, so we heard Mr. Beards long before we saw him.

"What's that buzzing noise?" said the Valkyrie.

"Could it be Mr. Beards's airship?"

"Too loud for one of his dirigibles," Mr. Scant said, standing and looking to the skies.

The noise became louder and louder, like some immense and terrible hornet, until we saw its source.

"Is that one of those aeroplanes?" said Mr. Jackdaw.

"Two," said Mr. Jackdaw.

"Do you think that's Mr. Beards?" I said.

"It would seem so."

And indeed it was. A small coastal road seemed an absurd place to land an aeroplane, but that's what happened. A flying machine bumped and screeched upon landing, coming to a halt, and another followed it.

The aeroplanes were not like the ones I had seen

in the newspapers, with two sets of wings above and below. Instead they had only one pair of wings each. Solid wings too, made of wood and polished like furniture. The planes looked as though they couldn't possibly stay in the air. Their tails were long and thin, composed of nothing more than a wooden frame that you could see right through. It appeared to be about as sturdy as a spider's web. Nonetheless, these machines had conveyed Mr. Beards to us, presumably all the way from London.

When Mr. Beards heaved himself out of the box he had been sitting in and removed his goggles, he looked as hale and hearty as I had ever seen him. He was out of breath, and his round belly seemed to weigh him down as he stumbled over to us, but I couldn't recall another time Father's friend had smiled like this. The other pilot stepped more gracefully from the other identical aeroplane, dressed in a striking purple flight suit and long leather boots.

"My dear Master Oliver!" Mr. Beards said, holding up his hands for an embrace, which he caught me in before I could quite understand what was going on. After chuckling and slapping my shoulder for a while, he stepped back and said, "Why, I've never felt so alive! What a time we live in. What a thrill!

Getting my flying license was a matter of short hops here and there between fields and air bases. But taking one of these beauties out over the Irish Sea and coming in to land in a city like this . . . Why, it makes ballooning seem about as interesting as a game of lawn bowls."

"Thank you for coming, Mr. Beards."

"Oh, my pleasure." He turned to the other pilot walking over. "A real pleasure, wouldn't you say, Miss Quimby?"

I looked in surprise at the pilot in purple. Somehow I had expected a second Mr. Beards. Now that she had taken off her goggles, I saw that she was instead a woman. She stood tall and confident with a young, healthy face and ready smile.

"A pleasure indeed," she answered in an American accent. She removed her glove so that she could shake our hands when Mr. Beards introduced her.

"This is Miss Harriet Quimby," he said, "critic and motion picture screenplay writer. Also the finest pilot I've ever had the privilege to meet!"

"Oh, please, you flatter me far too much," Miss Quimby said. She had a firm handshake and said hello to each of us as we were introduced, which was strangely endearing.

"We got your telegraph and thought this would be a fine chance for a flight," said Mr. Beards. "Miss Quimby is here from New York. She'll be the first woman ever to fly from England to France in an aeroplane."

"Any excuse for some practice," said Miss Quimby. "Especially when some generous soul is supplying the fuel!"

"So you write for movies *and* you're a pilot?" I said. "That's incredible!" And then I coughed because my voice had squeaked on the last word.

Miss Quimby smiled. "Anywhere I go, young people understand the cinema the best. I think it's because they care about what they're watching. Grown-ups who go to the theater, on the other hand, care much more about *being seen*. If you're ever in New York, I'll take you on a tour of our studio."

Meanwhile, Mr. Scant was serious as ever. "May I ask about the matter of getting to the Cape Colony?" he was saying to Mr. Beards.

"It's not a simple thing," Mr. Beards replied. "First, we'll go from here to our research facility on the Isle of Man. Then we can discuss it further. These aeroplanes only seat two at once, so we'll have to make a couple of trips." He tried to say it dolefully, but the way he smiled betrayed that he relished the prospect of further flights.

After some more discussion, we decided Mr. Scant and Mr. Jackdaw would go first. That way, they could begin planning the next steps in our journey. The two of them donned the extra flying jackets, hats, and goggles that Mr. Beards had brought for them, and off they went.

The Valkyrie and I were left standing by the town hall, and presumably she felt just as I did, totally unsure of what to say. We began to talk about getting some food. She said that since we were by the sea, they probably had some fine fish and chip shops about. When I said I had never tried fish and chips because Mother thought it was unhealthy, the Valkyrie sniffed, "You mean she thinks only poor people eat it." With that, we set off to find the nearest chip shop and give me my baptism by oiliness.

Our search didn't take long, and we stopped at a shop on a corner not far away. Knowing that the Valkyrie wasn't as wealthy as our family, I gave her some coins from my pocket.

"I'll take it for your half, but I can pay for my own," she said.

We sat on a little bench inside the shop while the shopkeeper prepared our meal. As the air filled with hissing and sizzling, I remarked that there was something fun about being able to hear your food cooking.

The meal didn't look very appetizing when it arrived—in all shades of brown—but I had to admit that when the fish, potato, and white sauce I didn't know the name of all mixed together, it was a very fine sensation.

Soon I was sated. "I can't eat the rest," I said apologetically.

"Give it here, then," said the Valkyrie. "No point it going to waste."

Another customer regarded us with curiosity as he waited for his order, looking up and down at our expensive clothes. "Aren't yez a bit fancy for a place such as this?" he rumbled at us.

"Not too fancy to give you a smack around the head," said the Valkyrie, and the man decided to whistle to himself rather than risk saying more.

After we finished eating, we returned to the town hall, and Mr. Beards and Miss Quimby returned not long after that. There was a bit of a problem when we found the Valkyrie couldn't fit into the flight jacket

Miss Quimby had brought. Mine was too big, but that was less of an issue.

"Never mind about it," said the Valkyrie. "My skin's tougher than a flimsy jacket anyway."

"Well, just put it over yourself like a blanket," said Miss Quimby. "You'll regret it if you don't." She handed us both our pairs of goggles. "Now let's hurry. If we don't get back by the time it gets dark, we'll be in hot water and no mistake."

And so it was that I had my first ride in an aeroplane. The craft was quite unlike a balloon or a dirigible, especially when leaving the ground. Rather than rising up gently, the machine seemed to take to the air by wrenching itself free of gravity. My insides felt as if they'd been left behind for a moment and had to race to catch up. But the scene below was very beautiful indeed, the buildings shrinking away, the sea and hills rushing in to show us how small human life truly was.

My pilot was Miss Quimby. She tried to shout back a few conversation points, but I couldn't hear her at all over the roar of the propeller, so I just said I was sorry and concentrated on the view. This was a fine way to travel, and faster than even a motorcar, but if Miss Quimby would be breaking some sort of record for simply going from England to France, I couldn't see how we could fly all the way to Africa. Which was a pity. The aeroplane's wooden seats were small and simple, but something about the judder of the engine was strangely comfortable.

I leaned back and, for the first time in weeks, relaxed. Clouds hovered above me, alongside me, all around me. I was suspended in the air, and the only things that kept me from falling to my death were the plane's wooden frame and the combustion engine that propelled us forward. It was about the most dangerous place I could imagine being, yet I felt completely serene.

I closed my eyes, at peace.

XX

To the Cape

I woke up to people laughing at me.

"That's Sandleforth's son, all right," I heard Mr. Beards say.

I opened my eyes and groped in confusion at whatever was strapped to my face. Flight goggles. Then I remembered where I was.

"I'm pleased you were able to relax in such a trying situation, Master Oliver," said Mr. Scant. I sat up but winced. I had drifted off in an awkward position, against the side of the aeroplane's wooden frame, and now my back ached.

"How on Earth did you sleep through the landing?" said the Valkyrie. "The way up was frightening enough, but the way down made me think my days were numbered. Maybe yours wasn't as bumpy as mine."

"Give the boy space," Miss Quimby was saying. "He might have fainted because of the thin air up there. Are you feeling all right, Master Oliver?"

"Yes, thank you, Miss Quimby," I said, pushing myself to my feet. "I think I did just fall asleep."

"I don't think we have anything to worry about," Mr. Jackdaw said, helping lift me down and then clapping a hand on my shoulder. "Stiff upper lip and a good constitution, that's the British way."

"I think it's very sweet that you could sleep in a place like that," said Miss Quimby.

"I'd prefer 'fearless' to 'sweet,'" I mumbled, which only made her laugh again.

We had flown to a small airfield on the Isle of Man, in between England and Ireland. Specifically to one of the research sites Mr. Beards's old company had set up, which I supposed made it one of my father's research sites now. We passed a number of balloons and dirigibles as we made our way from the airfield to what looked like a huge warehouse.

Inside, Mr. Beards confirmed there was no way to reach the Cape Colony by airship, the method Mr. Scant and I had used for our trip to China.

"As you fly south, the temperature becomes a huge problem," he said by way of explanation. "The issue isn't so much the extreme heat in the daytime—though it *would* be extremely unpleasant flying over the Sahara—but rather the depths of cold we would have to endure. I have faith that the machines would survive. But the passengers? Of that I am much less certain. There is also nowhere south of Cairo where we could refuel, nor a source of the hydrogen you would need to do so."

"So our only option is by sea?" said Mr. Scant. "Perhaps we can try to charter a vessel that could get us to Cape Town before the Binns boy. But time is of the essence, and we're well behind him."

"Now hold on just a moment," said Mr. Beards. He had put on little round spectacles and looked far sprightlier than I ever remembered him. "My dirigible business may only be a small part of Sandleforth's empire, but I still have my ways. While we may not be able to fly a balloon over the whole of Africa, that doesn't mean there's nothing at all we can do. If speed is of the essence, I'm sure I can come up with a route."

He led us to a large map laid out on a table. Various pins were stuck in it with bits of string running between them. He'd also arranged pairs of compasses, pencils, and what looked like the checkers from a backgammon board to mark different points around the world.

"From here," Mr. Beards continued, "we can take a dirigible to the secret airfield in Malta where my old friend Colonel Templer is developing airships for the navy. Now, this is very hush-hush business, so none of you heard about it from me. Even those of you who may have already known about it."

He gave Mr. Jackdaw a pointed look, and it struck me that perhaps Mr. Beards wasn't quite the harmless old coot I had always thought he was.

"I have a fair amount of equipment of my own there," Beards continued, "and Templer owes me a favor or two. From Malta, we load a collapsible balloon onto a steamer. And this we take down the Suez Canal. The balloon won't be a dirigible or anything of that sort, but it should serve your purposes.

"We can stop at Aden and Mombasa to resupply or hire a faster steamer, then continue to Madagascar and launch the balloon from the ship. That will take you where you need to go. I'll help with the launch, but you'll have to return by more conventional means. With the route before you, I guarantee you'll beat any liner that left today *or* yesterday, probably by quite some time."

"Malta, Aden—and then Mombasa?" Mr. Scant said, following the route on the large map. As everyone leaned in to try to make sense of the journey, Mr. Beards turned to Miss Quimby and clasped her hands. "I'm sorry, my dear, but I think I will have to miss your grand feat. I'm needed here."

"You're all quite mad," Miss Quimby said with a smile. "But that's why you're my friend, after all. I'll send you a postcard from France."

"It will be a treasure for me," Mr. Beards replied, "and I'm sure it will be in all the newspapers."

Mr. Jackdaw looked skeptical. "You're proposing we take an airship, then a steamer that can take us the full length of the African continent, and then a balloon . . . but that it will be faster than the commercial route Binns will be on?"

"Certainly. The portions by steamer will be the same speed as young Aurelian's vessel, but in the air, we'll be faster. The boy likely won't be travelling directly to Cape Town either. He may have to spend some days at a port, waiting for a second boat. There are not so many ships sailing directly to Africa."

"What's in it for you, though?" the Valkyrie asked. "The airship, privately-chartered steamers, a balloon to just abandon when we get there. That's a lot of expense. Even if you're a friend of the Diplexitos, why would you do it?"

Mr. Beards took a moment to clean his glasses before finally saying, "I suppose you wouldn't quite believe me if I said it's the adventure of flying. The truth is, Aurelian's father, the elder Binns, was my close friend and my business partner for many years. The boy—I held him in my arms before he could walk, before he could speak. I went to his christening, bought him toys for his birthday. And I was deceived.

"Nothing in all that time led me to understand what sort of person Binns—or his wife Thomasina, or the boy—was underneath. I was the one betrayed, but in truth I feel I let everybody down. An old fool, not suspecting a thing. And I suppose I never meant enough to Roland for him to share his plans with me either. That he was this master thief, this Ruminating Claw. I hadn't the faintest idea of the truth of it. And in a small way, I suppose, I want to make amends."

A short silence followed. Troubled, I said, "Mr. Beards, I think you should really know—"

Mr. Scant interrupted me: "You have no reason for a guilty conscience."

"Hear, hear," said Mr. Jackdaw. "But if you do this, I know all of us will be eternally grateful to you. And as the government expands its interest in airships, if you find yourself wanting more involvement . . . perhaps something can be arranged."

"I should like that," said Mr. Beards.

Mr. Scant interjected again. "How soon can we leave?"

"Well, we have a lot of arrangements to make, and I'll have to get in touch with Templer, but I see no reason we couldn't depart first thing in the morning."

The first arrangement Mr. Beards made involved a call to a local inn, which had several rooms open for the night. So after saying goodbye to Miss Quimby and wishing her well for her historic flight, we retired there. I ordered a plate of cheese and crackers to eat in the bar area, which—the bar, not the plate—was rather dusty and cluttered with old-fashioned furniture that sprouted fringing like dead trees sprout fungus. Mr. Beards and Mr. Jackdaw continued to plan for our journey, so I ate with Mr.

Scant and the Valkyrie. Mr. Scant had a brandy, and the Valkyrie some red wine. I opted for pressed apple juice.

"Nice to have a quiet moment after everything that's happened," I said. "I suppose we had some time while waiting for Mr. Beards and Miss Quimby in their aeroplanes, but that wasn't what I would call relaxing."

"I wouldn't call this relaxing either," said the Valkyrie. "Waiting and relaxing are different things."

"Why did you stop me telling Mr. Beards the truth?" I asked Mr. Scant.

"It's complicated," he replied.

"How is it complicated?"

The Valkyrie laughed a little. "When adults say it's complicated, what they mean is that it's too difficult to explain."

Mr. Scant bristled. "How would it have helped us, telling Mr. Beards all our secrets?"

"It would have helped him understand everything that's happened," I said. "He's given us so much, and I feel like we're lying to him."

"We can't risk any setbacks right now," Mr. Scant said. "He could feel betrayed enough to rescind his offer of help. If you want to tell him, feel free to do so after all this is over."

"I don't want him to know I used to do the Woodhouselee Society's dirty work and stop me from helping you," said the Valkyrie. "Actually, now that I think of it, that might have been a good way to get out of this."

At what must have been a wounded look from me, she sighed. "I suppose part of me wants to just go home and forget all about these last few days. That's normal, isn't it?"

"That's normal," I said. "I bet even Mr. Scant feels like that. Right, Mr. Scant?"

Mr. Scant ignored me. "We need to contact your father," he said. "This wasn't the plan."

"Sailing off to the United States, sailing off to the Union of South Africa," I said. "Is it so different?"

"The journey may not be, but the destinations, certainly. You've never been to the Cape Colony. I have. It's a dangerous place. And things have only got worse since I left. You saw the problems that emerged from a European presence in China. They are nothing compared to what happened in the Cape. Imagine men and women expected to toil in the darkness of a mine to make a man from London or Amsterdam richer than he already is. How do you suppose they feel?"

I was taken aback. "They must be angry."

Mr. Scant smiled for a moment, but there was no happiness in it.

"Once, I thought we brought enlightenment with us. That our cathedrals and our factories meant progress. Civilization. But to the man down in the mine, praying today won't be the day a collapsing mineshaft claims him, I don't suppose that makes a jot of difference. He's not a slave, true, but the mine's owner may take away his freedoms more subtly, by law. And even if the miner is the luckiest of the men like him that day and unearths the greatest diamond ever found—it is plucked from his hands and he's paid the same as any other day. Just enough that he and everyone he knows is kept under control. The control of a man like Basil Fields, who becomes a hero to his Empire, his name given someday to a town, a city, a whole plundered country."

There was a stunned silence for a few moments. before we disbanded for the night.

"You certainly have strong feelings about this," the Valkyrie said.

"Yes," Mr. Scant said, finishing his brandy. "Yes, I do."

We departed the next morning. From somewhere about the inn, the Valkyrie had procured a plain blouse and men's trousers, which looked to be much more comfortable than her disguise from the *Titanic*. Mr. Jackdaw told her she was "a vision of loveliness," and she snorted out a strange laugh.

The dirigible we boarded was much larger than the airship Mr. Scant and I had ridden to Shanghai. It could have been a suit of armor for an enormous fish. A pointed nose stretched out from the front end of the craft, while at the back end were little fins. We entered the gondola at bottom, and several of Mr. Beards's colleagues began to unload the ballast from a separate compartment beneath the dirigible. With none of the fanfare of the launch of the *Titanic*, Mr. Beards took us up into the skies.

We spent the first day travelling to Malta—still in Europe, Mr. Scant informed me, but not far from Africa's northern coast. We arrived there later than planned, at the last light of day, though a series of electrical lights guided us down safely. I was very eager to get out of the gondola while Mr. Beards met his friend Colonel Templer. Mr. Scant was making me study physics, while the Valkyrie kept reading aloud passages from a dreadful romance novel whenever the book's dashing Russian prince did something impressive. Mr. Jackdaw enjoyed trying to find fault with all of the prince's gestures, which put the Valkyrie in a huff.

We stayed on uncomfortable army bunk beds that night, and dinner was a bland beef stew with stodgy bread, but we were glad of the hospitality. Colonel Templer was a jolly soul with a waxed moustache and shiny bald head, and he told of his exploits during the second Boer War long into the night.

"For men in service, our utmost priority is to protect British souls," Colonel Templer concluded. "War is coming to Europe, and the moment we become weak is the moment we are snuffed out."

I expected Mr. Scant to be scowling, but he only looked at the ground and seemed to nod just a little.

The next day, we headed to a beautiful dock on Malta's shore, where the sea seemed to be strewn with a million glistening diamonds. How simple life would be, I thought, if I could have plucked one out to take back to London. We boarded an ugly steamship but one large enough to store our balloon for the final leg of our journey and the canisters of hydrogen we'd need to fill it. Mr. Beards said his goodbyes before we embarked, as he intended to stay with his friend to learn about the latest developments in ballooning. He also left us with strict instructions on how to use the small balloon, but Mr. Scant said he had experience.

The captain of the steamer, Captain Owen, was a very serious man who told me at once that he detested children. Though I said I would try not to disappoint him, he turned away and never spoke another word to me directly. He and his crew stayed close to the coastline until we reached the Suez Canal. We were in Africa—Egypt, to be precise. And all at once the air seemed to become much hotter. Sandy desert hemmed in the long, straight passage of water, as if the land was forever trying to quench its thirst, yet was never quite able to reach.

We next traversed the Red Sea. At first it was pleasant voyage. I lay with my shirt open, fanning myself. But soon I began to long for the frigid darkness of the Ice House. After two days, we stopped for supplies in Aden. It was a city I had never heard of—apparently a part of India, even though India was hundreds of miles away. A kind of mountain loomed over the port. Mr. Jackdaw told me it was once a volcano, and the city itself seemed to have been carved out of the rock that poured down in a great eruption long ago.

We didn't have much time in Aden, but we disembarked for long enough to have lunch at the city's "Steamer Point." The little port town housed a number of shops and restaurants run by British people. We were even able to eat lamb chops with potatoes— a rather strange experience, under the heavy sun of the Middle East. Throughout Steamer Point, men in long robes and colorful turbans nodded to us politely, some coming to see if they could sell us cloths and jewels, but we didn't have anything to pay them with.

In Mombasa, British East Africa, our next port of call, we learned of some grave news. Disaster had befallen the RMS *Titanic*. Approaching the United States of America, the liner had struck an iceberg and sunk under the sea, with thousands lost. I thought of all the faces I had seen, all the people I had smiled at, and wondered how many of them had been rescued—if any at all.

"Do you suppose it was Aurelian's doing?" I said. "Was it a trap for us?"

"I think not," Mr. Scant said, grim-faced. "It doesn't strike me as something he could possibly have arranged, even had he wanted to murder all those people just to get to us."

"He could have laid a curse on the boat," said the Valkyrie. "His mother would often put hexes on people."

"Curses don't work," said Mr. Scant. "May God rest all those souls."

Mombasa was a busy port city with a railway, though nobody seemed to know where the railway went. Since we'd arrived on a steamship, people at the port expected we'd have much to trade. Everyone we met was surprised when we said we were only passing through. Brightly colored houses filled the city, all yellows and blues, which Mr. Jackdaw said was the Portuguese style. "The Portuguese came and took it from the local people, then the Arab sultans came and took it from the Portuguese," he explained as we walked through a busy market.

"Don't tell me," I said, "we British came and took it from the sultans."

"Not quite. First the Portuguese got control again. Then the sultans once again took it back. But they were close allies of the British at that point, so they leased the city to our own East Africa Company. No violence involved."

"Not by us, anyway," Mr. Scant said.

"Not this time," said Mr. Jackdaw, with his usual bright smile.

"Not yet."

Before we left Mombasa, I spent some time walking around the city's port area. Stopping at a market stall, I ate a curious dish with scraps of pork and many beans in a thick, flavorsome sauce. It was unlike anything I had eaten before, and though I wasn't sure about it at first, by the time I finished my plate I wanted more.

We returned to the boat with a newspaper from England, which I read again and again. There was also mention of Miss Quimby, on page six. She had completed her flight to France, the first woman to do so in an aeroplane. But I wasn't sure anyone would ever learn of her feat. The paper gave it only a little space beside all the information about how the unsinkable came to be sunk.

After another two days, we reached our destination, off the coast of Madagascar. The waters were calm, and the heat had become less maddening as we had traveled south. The night before, I had been almost entirely unable to sleep, with the heat, the motion of the waves, the sound of the steamship's engine, and especially my thoughts of the ocean liner plunging into the depths. So I struggled to stay awake as the balloon was inflated. This new one stood somewhere between a dirigible and a hot air balloon, from what I could tell. It didn't have the rigid frame of a dirigible, but despite the burner at its center, it was much more sophisticated than a simple balloon. And from the crates Mr. Beards had left us, we could assemble a whole gondola rather than just a basket.

"This is it, then," said Mr. Scant. "If anyone wants to turn back, this is the time."

"There's no turning back," I said. "Not now that we've come this far."

"Quite right," said Mr. Jackdaw.

"I wouldn't mind going back to Mombasa," the Valkyrie said. "I liked it there. But I gave my word, and I'll help you until the end."

"It may have been peaceful so far," Mr. Scant said, his hand on the bag containing his golden claw, "but the Cape is another world altogether."

"I'm not afraid," I said. "Let's go."

XXI
Arrival

Mr. Scant and Mr. Jackdaw took on the task of navigating us, while the Valkyrie and I stayed at opposite corners of the ship's front side, looking out of the large windows.

"Do you remember our last encounter in a balloon?" I said to the Valkyrie.

"All too well. I may not have shown it, but at the time, I was terrified I'd be carried off into the sky."

"Are you afraid of heights?"

"Not particularly. I'm afraid of falling to my death."

"I suppose that's normal," I said.

The Valkyrie looked out to the horizon. There was no sign of land yet. All we could see was a deep, shifting blue for miles ahead.

"I've always been fascinated by air balloons, to tell you the truth," the Valkyrie said. "A balloon hangs in the air, refusing to accept that it should fall. And we hang underneath it like puppets held up on strings. Maybe that fits me well, eh? I'm not a real Valkyrie, just a sort of puppet. But I'm all done with letting other people pull the strings."

She looked over at me to see what I made of that.

"What on Earth are you going on about?" I said with a smile.

The Valkyrie's laugh was loud enough I felt sure it changed the course of the balloon just a little.

"I think you know," she said. "And if you really don't, you'll see when we get to where we're going."

When we first landed at the Cape Colony, I thought we were only stopping to rest or find supplies. There was nothing to see in the place where we'd touched down. Only dust and a few skinny trees and a trail toward what may have been a village off in the distant haze. So Mr. Scant surprised me when he said we were waiting for the balloon to collapse.

"Why do we need it to deflate?" I asked.

"I'm not just going to leave it on the roadside," said Mr. Scant. "It could cause a lot of problems if it blows into a field. But if we pack it up, some lucky passer-by will probably take it to be sold. I had Mr. Beards write a note saying they have permission to do so."

"But don't we need it to carry on?"

"No," said Mr. Scant. "From here, we walk."

"But this can't be Cape Town," I said. "There's nothing here."

"It's not Cape Town," said Mr. Scant. "We were never going to Cape Town. That's may be where Aurelian's steamer was going, but Hunter said he was taking the diamond *home*. That doesn't mean Cape Town or his hometown in America or even in the Transvaal where the diamond was first found. He means Kimberley. We have a much better chance of finding and stopping them there, where just maybe I can ask some old friends for favors."

"It's probably changed a lot since you were last here, old bean," Mr. Jackdaw said.

"No doubt," said Mr. Scant. "And not for the better."

"Why did we have to land so far from the city?" I asked.

"We don't want to draw too much attention," said Mr. Scant.

After taking the time to get all the balloon parts back into their crates, we began the walk toward the distant smudge of buildings.

"I've never seen such an empty place," said the Valkyrie.

"Be on your guard nonetheless," said Mr. Scant.

"This is still British territory, isn't it?" I asked.

"That doesn't mean it's safe," said Mr. Scant.

"Even for Britons?"

"Even for armed Britons."

The trudge down the road was not pleasant. The heat outdid any summer's day in England, and a profusion of flies filled the air around us. To the eyes, the nose, the tongue, everything was unendingly dry. The rest of us removed our jackets and loosened our shirts in the heat, but Mr. Scant doggedly kept his black jacket and ribbon bowtie on.

The Kimberley outskirts came upon us all at once. I had indeed underestimated the kind of a place this was. It wasn't so different from a town back in England, with shops and houses and even a tram.

"I wasn't sure whether it would be all shanties or whether it would be like Shanghai," I said. "It's not like either."

"The people don't look very happy to see us,"

said the Valkyrie. She had taken her leather satchel off her back in case she needed her cleavers.

The locals I saw mostly closed their shutters if we noticed them inside the buildings, or they passed by with their heads low if they were on the road. Some glanced at us furtively, with anger in their eyes.

"They're very different from the people in Mombasa," I observed.

"Does that surprise you?" said Mr. Jackdaw. "It oughtn't to. Would you be surprised if the people you meet in Paris are different from those you meet in Prague?"

"It's not because this is another country," I said, a little defensively. "It's . . . I don't know, really."

"Consider this," Mr. Jackdaw said. "Mombasa existed before the British, before the Portuguese or the sultans. It will go on existing after any of them are gone. New Rush was nothing before the diamonds. Almost every man here has come for one of two reasons—to labor in the pits or to profit from that labor."

"I still don't understand why Aurelian would come here," I said. "Will there really be people here who can buy the diamond?"

"Enough buyers, certainly," Mr. Scant said. "But

more than that, I suspect this is Aurelian making a statement. This is not about money to him. It's about defying the Crown. But I also think this is aimed at me."

"You? Why?"

Of course, Mr. Scant would say no more about it.

Once we reached a certain part of town, he was increasingly on his guard. The others probably didn't notice, but I began to see him scrutinize every face that passed. We saw more and more people of other nationalities, some whites and occasionally people from India too. The whites were almost all well-dressed, followed by dark-skinned attendants who were also much better-dressed than the rest of the townspeople. Mr. Scant was my family's attendant, and people usually treated him with respect. But I wondered if these men could say the same.

"They have electric street lamps," Mr. Jackdaw observed, sounding impressed.

"They've had them for thirty years," said Mr. Scant. "You need to stop thinking of Kimberley as some backward village. It may not be Oxford Street, but this is a city built for function. If any latest technology has a use in the mining trade, you can expect to find it here."

"*Has* it changed much since you were last here?" I asked.

"Yes. Everything is more developed. A lot more people, a lot more buildings. I read that they have a Savoy Hotel now. But the feeling—it feels just the same as it used to."

"Where are we going?"

"This way."

I was reminded of Shanghai as we walked further into the city. Kimberley had more markets, more large buildings, but also piles of refuse and a number of large tents that seemed to have been set up as permanent lodgings. We began to pass people sitting in doorways, watching us with doleful eyes.

"That poor fellow has no arms," I said, spotting a man sitting at the dividing point between two stores. The man's sleeves were tied off at his shoulders, his head mostly bald but for a few patches of tightly curled white hair that stood out against his dark skin.

"He probably lost them in the mines," said Mr. Scant.

"What does he do to live?" I said.

"Whatever he can, I suppose."

I paused. "They use pounds and pence here, don't they? I want to give him some money."

"He doesn't have a bowl," said Mr. Jackdaw. "He's not a beggar. You might insult him."

"Shouldn't we at least ask him?" I said.

"Are you going to help every injured man you see?" Mr. Scant said. "It will take a lifetime. And when you help the last man, all the rest will need your help again."

"I'm not trying to change the world," I said. "I just want to help this man, right now, today. If he wants me to help."

Mr. Scant nodded, so I finally approached the man. "Hello," I said, squatting down in front of him.

"Who's this?" said the man.

"My name's Oliver," I said. "What's yours?"

"They call me Sam," said the man. He had an accent, but it was not difficult to understand him.

"Mr. Sam?"

He laughed. "Sure, Mr. Sam."

"Did you lose your arms in the mines?" I asked.

For some reason, this question seemed to cheer him up. "That I did. What, do I look scary to you?" He laughed. "Don't be scared of me. Broke them because of some rocks knocking down a place where we stood. Doc said they have to come off. So here I sit and help where I can. I'm lucky. I got my brother.

He runs this shop. I spot the regulars coming and tell him what he should get ready for them."

"Was it very painful, losing your arms?"

"Oh, pain like you never knew." He laughed again.

I couldn't help but smile. "Why are you laughing?"

"Now there's no more pain. When I remember that pain, and I remember I don't have the pain now, well, I feel okay. Only bad part is when I get an itch."

"I wondered if you wanted some money," I said. "I know you're not begging, but I thought it might help."

"Oh, now there's big talk from the young man! Sometimes people say to me they want to give me money. They feel sorry for me, I know. I know. So I'll tell you the same thing I tell them. If you want to pay me for a job, I'll do it. I won't say no, but I'd rather be useful."

That sounded reasonable. I stood up and turned to the adults. "Mr. Scant?"

"Yes?"

"Where are we going?" I asked. "What road?"

"Well, for now we'll go to the Kimberley station. Our final destination isn't far from there."

I turned back to the man I had been speaking to. "Will you take us to the station for sixpence, Mr. Sam?"

"I don't see why not," he said graciously. He got up and told his brother in the shop that he had a little job to do. "This way," he said, and began to walk ahead of us.

I went to join the others. "I'm sure you know the way, but I just thought it was a good thing to do," I said to Mr. Scant.

"No doubt," said Mr. Scant. "There's nothing wrong with helping where you can."

Emboldened, I went to talk to Mr. Sam. He told me about life in the mines, which sounded terrible. "Children used to work in the mines in England," I told him.

"Oh, they put a stop to that there, did they?" said Mr. Sam.

"I think so."

He laughed. "You don't know."

We reached the station before long. As promised, I slipped the sixpence into the little bag Mr. Sam had strung about his neck, and he soon went running back to where we had met. "He was a nice fellow," I told the others. "You should have spoken with him."

"Next time," said Mr. Scant.

Mr. Jackdaw wasn't smiling his usual smile. "Are you done playing savior from on high? We're here with a mission—to recover that diamond."

"He took us where we were meant to go," I replied. "Maybe it made us quicker."

There was a pause, and then the smile reappeared. "Forgive my being brusque," Mr. Jackdaw said, mopping his brow with a handkerchief from his pocket. "A little too hot for me, I think."

"You can say that again," said the Valkyrie. She shaded her eyes with one hand as she walked, as if doing some kind of salute. "I'll need some water soon, if it doesn't slow us down too much."

"Oh, but of course refreshments will be necessary in conditions such as these!" Mr. Jackdaw said. "Your comfort is of paramount importance to me."

We stopped at a little counter in the station to try red bush tea. We took it without milk or sugar, as was the custom, but it tasted smooth and delicious to my parched throat. Following that, we continued on past the other side of the city's railroad tracks.

"Where are we actually going?" said Mr. Jackdaw. "I don't suppose all underground diamond sales take place at the same address?"

"No," said Mr. Scant. "The one who has the diamond is my old teacher, Hunter the Just. We're going to find *him*. And we'll do that by speaking with the one person I'm certain will know where he is."

"Wait, are we going to the school?" I asked. "It's been years. Are you sure everything will be the same?"

"I'm sure," said Mr. Scant. "That's the way she is."

"She might not even still be alive," I said.

"That just goes to show you've never met her."

"Who are you talking about?" Mr. Jackdaw asked.

"Another old friend."

The school, like most of the other buildings in this city, was small and simple. It stood only a single story high, not counting its hipped roof. Inside, it couldn't have fit more than four or five classrooms, if there was an assembly hall and a staff room as well. A wall with iron railings ran around the place, but nothing in the school's arched gateway served to stop us entering.

"It's bigger than it used to be," said Mr. Scant.

The hour was late, most likely too late for schoolchildren, and indeed I thought the staff might have gone home as well. But Mr. Scant strode confidently to the front entrance and opened the school door. It was a simple wooden door with a stained glass window, small enough that everyone but me had to duck to step inside.

"Suthu!" he called. "Are you here? I need to speak with you. Suthu!"

A creak came from somewhere inside the place. A moment later, a woman appeared, her mouth agape. She was small, only an inch or two taller than me, with short hair—still dark, despite her being sixty or so. Around her neck hung a pair of thin-rimmed glasses. Her skin was lighter than Mr. Sam's, with a band of freckles across her nose, and something about her face was girlish and mischievous.

Slowly but steadily, she walked up to Mr. Scant, who cleared his throat and said, "I hope you remember me. It's H—"

That was as far as he got before her fist sent him crashing to the floor.

XXII
The Big Hole

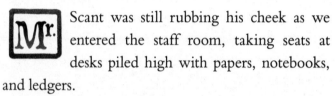 Scant was still rubbing his cheek as we entered the staff room, taking seats at desks piled high with papers, notebooks, and ledgers.

"Let's start again from the beginning," Mr. Scant's old friend said as she took her place at a desk that faced all the others. She addressed us just as she would a classroom full of children, and if this was the staff room, she probably did the same for everyone who worked for her. "My name is Mrs. Nosuthu Hunter. I am the headmistress of this school, which is the Kimberley Unified School. Now, if you would be so kind, I would like you to introduce yourselves."

She spoke clearly and carefully, in the manner of one who had learned English to fluency but never adopted the relaxed carelessness of a native speaker.

Her speech was perfect like a crystal vase, with no softness to it.

We introduced ourselves one by one, Mr. Jackdaw identifying himself as such, presumably to keep things simple. Mr. Scant said nothing, as expected. The Valkyrie slipped in an apology. A second after Mrs. Hunter had punched Mr. Scant, she had surged forward and wrapped a hand around the older woman's throat, but Mr. Scant called her off.

"I accept your apology," Mrs. Hunter told the Valkyrie. "And I offer an apology of my own—to you, Heck. I ought not to have attacked you, so I am sorry."

"Apology accepted," Mr. Scant said, but his hand stayed on his cheek.

"It was not ladylike, I suppose," Mrs. Hunter went on. "But then today I don't feel much like being a lady."

"Please, Mrs. Hunter—why did you punch Mr. Scant?" I asked.

"He has brought back many strong emotions from my past," she said, shifting in her chair with a dissatisfied expression. "When we hoped for his help, he left us. When we believed he would return to aid us in our darkest times, he never came. He was the ghost that ran from us. The warrior who would no longer fight alongside us. A valuable link with the other side. He could have spoken on our behalf, and yet—"

"You knew I wasn't coming back," said Mr. Scant. "And I wouldn't have been able to change anything if I had. If the lot of you working together couldn't do anything, I wouldn't have made the slightest difference."

"I didn't strike you for failing to save us. I struck you for failing to even lend a hand."

Mr. Scant seemed to soften. He lowered his hand. "Was it very bad while I was away?"

"So very bad," said Mrs. Hunter. "Some of it, I am sure you know. But living here, it has been atrocious. Not every day, of course. The school brings me great happiness. You guessed, no doubt, that Bart and I married. We had no children, but being together has been blissful for the most part. In these walls and in our home, we have jolly old lives that I feel sure are better than your stuffy king's. But the fight Bart came here for—that fight was lost.

"The diamonds," she continued, "they changed everything. Now that devil Basil Fields owns almost all of this country. Now the government says if your land is not worth £75, you no longer have the right to vote. Before it was £25, and many of us outside white communities met that requirement, but triple that? The door was shut to everyone I know. The law was *calculated* to shut us out. That Fields's accursed South African Union Party has sewed up our mouths so they can laugh at our silence."

Her lips twitched a little as she paused, polishing the lenses of her glasses with a cloth. None of us dared interrupt.

"But that was only the beginning. If you cannot read, you cannot vote. If your tribe owns your land, not you, it does not count toward your £75. Bart came here to live in a land where all men had equal voting rights. Now it's a land where nobody even hides any more the truth of the matter. Men born half a world away, like you, control the law. And we who were born here, or brought here by force, can only submit. Before long they will stop pretending it's anything to do with money or land and will outright decree that only whites can vote. Just as it is in the rest of this Union of South Africa, so it will be here in the Cape."

"But that makes no sense," I said. "It's only going to make people want to fight back."

"It gives Fields's party the power to throw anyone

who fights back into prison," said Mr. Jackdaw. "Control, that's what matters here."

"So that is what changed while you were away," said Mrs. Hunter. "Now, your turn to speak. Why are you here?"

"We're here about the hero," said Mr. Scant. "Your husband."

"Ha! You are disappointed I married him?"

"Of course not," he replied. "In fact your marriage is something I always hoped would happen. I'm disappointed I couldn't be at the wedding. But you know what he's done, what he's doing now?"

"We no longer talk as much as we once did," Mrs. Hunter said. "He goes away for weeks at a time. Continuing what the two of *you* started. And still fighting for the dream you once shared with him."

"Did he tell you where he went this time? What he went to do?"

"No," she said. "But I trust him. He still fights for this country. A country that is no more his homeland than it is yours, and yet *he* fights."

Mr. Jackdaw, perhaps growing anxious, spoke up next.

"Madam, your husband assisted in the theft of perhaps the most valuable jewel in the world, property of His Majesty himself. This is no small matter. I'm going to have to ask for your cooperation in recovering the diamond."

"One of Kimberley's diamonds?" said Mrs. Hunter. "I would never believe it. My Bart would never touch a diamond from these accursed mines."

"Well, not a Kimberley diamond exactly," said Mr. Jackdaw. "It was from up near Pretoria. The greatest diamond ever found."

Mrs. Hunter smiled slightly. "In that case, I suppose Bart might have had a hand in it."

Mr. Jackdaw's face went a little red. "Madam! I'm not sure you grasp the severity of this situation."

"Well, I'm not sure you grasp how little it means to me, your diamond *or* your king."

I decided this was my time to speak. "Do you have any idea when Mr. Hunter will return, or what he's going to do when he gets here?"

"My husband is not a man to break his word," Mrs. Hunter said. "He will continue what he started with his fellow *hero* so many years ago."

I looked at Mr. Scant in confusion, but he said nothing.

"Ah, I see how it is," said Mrs. Hunter. "You told them of your time here but not about what was *born* from it. You know, I feel like a walk. Will you all give me the pleasure of accompanying me?"

The Valkyrie turned to Mr. Jackdaw, that old fury in her eyes returning. "Why give her the chance to run? We could just twist what she knows out of her."

"Oh, worry ye not," said Mrs. Hunter. "I'll tell you what you need to know. Even where to find my husband when he arrives two days from now. But first, a walk."

Mrs. Hunter used a cane to walk outdoors. She didn't appear to need it very much but she seemed to enjoy waving it at us as she talked.

We walked the length of the road outside the school, then stepped onto a street busy with the cries of shopkeepers and the chatter of people going about their daily business.

"Where are we going?" I asked Mr. Scant.

"To the mines, I think," he replied.

"What did she mean about what was *born*?"

"She's taking pleasure in drawing out my past."

I resolved to wait and see what the mysterious old woman wanted to tell us. I noticed a peculiar trend as she walked through the town. Young children seemed to smile at the sight of her, often waving as she passed, but older children and adults gave her a wide berth. I wondered what made the difference.

Before long, we came to a road with shops and buildings on one side and very little on the other. No buildings or trees, only a mound of dry earth. Mrs. Hunter led us across the road and started up the mound, beginning to rely in earnest on her cane.

"The view is quite something," she said as she reached the top.

And so it was. Even as I stood still, I felt like I was falling.

The Big Hole of Kimberley was unlike anything I would have pictured before I saw it. If Mrs. Hunter had asked me to draw my idea of it, back in the staff room, I would have perhaps sketched a large well going down a great distance, or possibly a cave entrance that lead down into a great network of caves. Neither of which was anywhere near what I saw.

The whole earth opened up as though to swallow the entire city. The chasm that was the Big Hole gaped before me, crisscrossed with toothpick ladders and hair-thin pulley ropes. The number of lives that must have been lost in its teardrop shape was unfathomable.

"What do you think of that?" said Mrs. Hunter.

"It's incredible," I said. "Terrifying."

"And made by human hands," said Mrs. Hunter. "If they can find more diamonds by going deeper, then deeper they go. And around the edges, there are mineshafts you can't see from here, leading to all the ledges and different flat surfaces down there. If you're searching for my husband, that's where he will be. Not in the Big Hole, but in one of the holes leading off from it. And you have no hope whatsoever of finding him without me."

"Are you going to help us?" I said.

"That depends on whether or not you understand. Not about diamonds or stealing—I cannot say what the truth is there myself, and I don't particularly care. But about purpose. About what my husband and his apprentice over there vowed to do."

"And what was that?" I asked.

"We vowed to bring an end to the mining companies here," Mr. Scant said. "An end to the system that supported them."

"And how did you intend to achieve this?" said Mrs. Hunter.

"Through a society."

"A secret society," Mrs. Hunter added with a smile.

"To infiltrate the corridors of power," Mr. Scant said grimly. "To influence politicians. To take power *away* from the bloated leeches like the mining companies. To restore it to all the people."

"I cannot say precisely what my husband plans to do," Mrs. Hunter said with venom in her voice, "but I am certain, quite *certain*, that it will tear apart Fields's so-called South African Union Party. Pull apart the circles of power, end the cycle of easy deaths for stones. Isn't that what you founded it for, Scant? Your precious Woodhouselee Society?"

I had been looking into the hole when she spoke those words, and suddenly felt as though I were being pulled into it. I had to grab hold of Mr. Jackdaw's wrist to stop myself from falling.

"And now you're here to keep the change—the culmination of everything—from happening," Mrs. Hunter went on. "Finally, a chance to do what you set out to do all those years ago, you and my husband, and me too—don't forget me. But you're here to put a stop to it all. Shame on you, Heck Scant. Shame on you."

XXIII
Hunter the Just

If Mr. Scant had been quiet since his encounter with Bartholomew Hunter, now it was as though he had taken a vow of silence. Time passed more and more slowly as we waited for the arrival of Mr. Hunter. We took rooms in the local Savoy Hotel, which was far smaller than the name had led me to expect. I don't know if Mr. Jackdaw thought Mr. Scant needed space, but he put us all in separate quarters, which I thought was no help at all. Mr. Scant never answered my knocks.

Of course, I tried to get my mentor to explain what Mrs. Hunter's words all meant, but all he said was, "The Society that the Hunters and I devised here and the Society you and I fought against have nothing in common."

"So you admit you had a part in creating it?"

At that, he walked away.

During breakfast on our second day in Kimberley, I said, "The Society didn't just target Uncle Reggie because was a drunk, was it? It was because they knew he was your brother."

"No, that's not true," said Mr. Scant. "Not completely. Only Thomasina Binns knew of the connection, and she thought pressing Reginald would bring me back to the Society. It would have been her idea to target him, but she didn't tell her husband the true reason. He would have worried she wanted to replace him as leader with one of the founders. With me."

"I just don't believe this," I said. "It wasn't just here? You were part of the Society in England as well."

"Only at the very beginning. It makes no difference to what you and I are doing here and now. We need to concentrate on recovering this diamond."

Unsatisfied, I went to talk to Mrs. Hunter alone. I wanted to arrive after school had already finished, but I discovered it finished later in Kimberley than in England. Children were filing out of the little gate when I arrived. Pushing through them would be like trying to swim upstream, so I just waited. The schoolchildren were all different races, though mostly black, and I noticed that only very rarely were any of them talking to a child of a skin color different from their own.

When the gate was clear, I stepped inside and made my way to the staff room. A teacher I didn't recognize, a young African man with cropped hair, answered my knocks, so I said I'd like to talk to Mrs. Hunter.

"Who shall I say is asking?" he said.

"I'm Oliver Diplexito."

The man took a breath, then frowned. "You're gonna have to say that one more time."

"It's okay, Arnold. I know who this is." Mrs. Hunter stepped into the doorway. "Come. I live in an annex at the back of the building. We'll talk there."

She led me through the school's corridors to a locked door and—once we removed our shoes—a small but richly decorated living room. It was covered in greens and dark yellows, and on the wall hung a modern picture of dark figures dancing with an eagle.

"Sit, sit," said Mrs. Hunter. "The gray owl brought his owl chick with him. So similar in some ways, except that maybe the chick knows how to listen. What do you think of my school?"

"It seems nice."

"Not so big beside your Eton or your Rugby."

"I didn't think about how big it was," I said. "Honestly, I don't think I can say if it's a good or bad school when I've never seen what the lessons are like."

Mrs. Hunter made a steeple with her fingers. "Interesting answer. Did you talk with any of our students?"

"No, they were all on their way home. And I know *I* wouldn't stop to talk to someone I didn't know when I could be going home instead. Besides, I didn't know if they would talk to me anyway. I noticed they were staying in their groups. Everyone with the people who looked like them."

She nodded. "For the most part. There have always been divisions here, but never so much as there are now."

"I can tell. But the school still exists. They still have the chances to get to know one another if they want to. So it's not as divided as all that."

She lowered her hands and gave me a hard look. "Perceptive. Now why are you here?"

"You know why I'm here. To talk about your husband."

"How you have come to this land to expose him as a villain? To see him taken away in chains?"

"How can we expose him as a villain unless that's what he is?"

Mrs. Hunter leaned forward. "I don't presume to know your life, owl chick, or what Heck has done since he left this place. But I know he still believes that those who have been robbed are just and righteous when they take it back."

"That's not what Mr. Scant taught me."

"Explain."

"There's another step you missed," I said. "He didn't just take back what was stolen. He returned it to where it belonged and never asked for anything for himself."

"I don't know the details of what Hunter means to do. But I feel certain that same feeling is inside him too."

"Maybe in *him*," I said. "But I don't think the same can be said for the ones he's doing business with."

"All the same, my husband had to act. When the power of words is taken away from you, all that's left is the power of actions. Heck understood that once."

"They understood *each other* once," I said. "It's so sad they don't any more. I've never seen Mr. Scant so shaken as he has been since he saw your husband again. More than I want to see the diamond returned, I want them to be able to talk. Not fight, but talk."

Mrs. Hunter had steepled her fingers again. She rested her chin on her thumbs, looking at me from either side of her fingertips.

"Will you help me?" I said. "Not a trap or a quarrel, I promise. Just a meeting, so they can talk?"

"His train arrives tomorrow at eleven. The first thing he will do is come to me. Bring Heck here and they can talk. Bring your flock of owls and jackdaws, it's all the same. But if you try to double-cross us, I'll be ready for it."

We went to the school again the next day, this time during lessons, and found Mrs. Hunter teaching a class. She introduced us as "observers," and we stood at the back of the class as she taught a room of five- and six-year-olds how to spell the names of different animals. She was a patient and kind teacher but very firm. Two girls kept playing a game together even after she asked them to stop, so she sent them to stand facing the corners until they "learned to do as they were told."

At playtime, we tried to stay away from the children, but the Valkyrie fascinated them. The students came over cautiously at first, but then one took her hand and asked, "Why are you bigger than my mama?" That emboldened the rest.

"Are you a giant but not all grown up yet?"

"Do you know the strong lady from the circus?"

The Valkyrie tried to answer them, but soon there were so many questions nobody knew which one she was answering. After another minute of this, we had to pluck the children from her.

Around eleven o'clock, we headed back into Mrs. Hunter's classroom, and soon afterward Hunter the Just appeared. He stepped into the room without knocking, travel gloves in hand, and said, "There she is!" before walking over to his wife for a kiss. It was then that he noticed us.

"Just as you said, Husband, they came," Mrs. Hunter said.

He had expected us, I realized. But even so, Hunter the Just stared at us for a moment, his eyes wide, as if making calculations. Then he straightened up and turned on his heel, back the way he had come.

"Oh no you don't!" Mr. Jackdaw called after him. The children swiveled in their chairs to stare at the scene.

"Calm down, Mr. Jackdaw," I said. "We just want to talk."

But the others were already in pursuit. There was no choice. Even if we only wanted words with Mr. Hunter, we'd have to catch him first. But Mr. Jackdaw clearly wanted more than that, and I was beginning to fear I couldn't keep my promise to Mrs. Hunter.

Mr. Hunter didn't lead us far. He clearly only wanted us away from the children, and he stopped to wait in the empty assembly hall.

"We've got you now," said Mr. Jackdaw.

"You don't have anyone," Hunter shot back. He put his fingers to his mouth and made a loud, piercing whistle. At the sound, five other men came running into the hall, with skin as dark as Mr. Hunter's, all young and well-dressed, with nice clothes that made me think they were likely university students. They had us surrounded.

"So you really did beat us here," said Mr. Hunter. I realized I had forgotten he had an American accent. "The skinny kid said you would. I didn't doubt him, if we're being honest."

"We're here to stop you selling that diamond," said Mr. Scant.

"It doesn't belong to you," added Mr. Jackdaw. "It was gifted to His Majesty."

"And I'm sure His Majesty the King has many uses for it," Mr. Hunter said, "but our need is greater."

"To fund a criminal organization?" I said.

"Ah, yes," said Mr. Hunter. "That's all you think we're doing. Stealing a stone, selling it for profit. You don't understand what this diamond means."

"The blood and labor of the country's people," said Mr. Scant. "We do understand that. But this is only a small part of a bigger game. You're not seeing that. You think you're using Aurelian Binns, but he's manipulating you. If this theft becomes public knowledge, your situation here will only get worse. Binns will walk away with money and power, and you'll, what? Found a rebel state to fight against the greatest empire the world has ever seen? It's not the just way. It's not the hero's way."

"Gray, you never did understand," Mr. Hunter said, shaking his head as if Mr. Scant had said the wrong thing completely. "Men who rose to power on nothing but diamonds can be torn down with nothing but diamonds." From the pocket of his light waistcoat he withdrew a simple handkerchief. "Do you remember, when we were young, it was Basil and Hubert Fields with their gangs of thugs, forcing everyone else to give up their claims or face a beating? Hubert may be gone, but Basil runs the country now. Runs half the continent. And his South African Union Party controls the mines."

He unwrapped the handkerchief to reveal the full luster of the stone inside. "Except the mine where this came from. The Premier Mine. This diamond represents the weakness of the South African Union Party. It infuriates the men who run this city, this country, this whole continent. For all their influence, they've never been able to match up to this, this most perfect and beautiful of diamonds. They've never been able to buy out that one mine a few hundred miles northeast of here. And now the diamond's back with us. With our Society. You remember our Society, don't you, Gray?"

The men who had appeared when Mr. Hunter whistled stood behind him, ready to fight.

"We're selling it," he continued, "but on our terms. That's how it always should have been. We're selling it here, to a buyer in this country, proud of their roots. Not someone who wants it locked behind glass half a world away. And with the money we make, we'll take the power back from those men who want to see us made into livestock."

"You can't sell what doesn't belong to you," Mr. Jackdaw said through gritted teeth. "You will be marked as common thieves. And if they can't arrest you, they'll send an army to crush you."

"There are ways," said Mr. Hunter. "We have a document that shows the diamond was never truly gifted to the king. That was a forgery—the diamond in the sceptre was fake from the beginning. People will come to believe the real diamond has always been here. Our document's quite convincing. Nobody will be able to question it."

"The Crown examined the diamond," Mr. Jackdaw insisted. "They will know this story is false."

"I think the news will be very embarrassing for the royal jewelers. After all, their diamond is still in London, is it not? Still in the Tower, with visitors marveling over its beauty every day. What will they see when they examine it again, I wonder?"

Mr. Scant stepped forward. "Hunter, no justice can come from an alliance with a man like Binns. This is a crime. This is against the second principle of the Woodhouselee Society."

"What do I care about your principles?" Hunter said. "There are people who will benefit from this and people who lose nothing. I don't think there's anything more to say. Tomorrow, the exchange takes place, and there's no way you can stop it."

"You're not going anywhere," the Valkyrie said, pulling out her cleavers.

"We're not here to hurt anyone," said Mr. Scant.

"Then stand down," said Mr. Hunter. With that, he stepped out of the assembly room doors.

The five men Mr. Hunter had summoned knew what was happening. They probably didn't care whether we fought or not, but they were here to stall us.

"You're on the wrong path!" Mr. Scant yelled after Mr. Hunter, but Hunter gave no response. One man with a scar on his lip looked ready to fight. He walked forward with a hand up to block Mr. Scant's path, but before they could meet, Mr. Scant ducked down and swept the man's feet from under him.

That was the cue for a dance of chaos to begin. Three men went for the Valkyrie, who was running forward with her cleavers crossed in front of her. The fifth man headed straight for Mr. Jackdaw. I had sunk back, wary of who was going to come for me, but

I knew what I had to do. With Mr. Hunter's men distracted, I alone was able to slip out of the assembly hall to follow him.

Of all the skills I had learned from Mr. Scant, following others was the one we had worked on the most and which I felt I could do the best. Mr. Hunter was fast and had a head start, but that only made it easier to keep my distance and watch him from safe vantage points. Several times he turned around, and several times I ducked out of sight. I always waited twice as long as I felt I had to before looking out again.

I knew at once where we were going. Back to the Big Hole, to one of the mineshafts. Mrs. Hunter had said that was where the Society met. The Society, which I still could not believe Mr. Scant had founded. If I could only see which mineshaft Mr. Hunter entered, even if there was a labyrinth within the hole, it was better than not knowing.

Tailing the hero became more difficult when we reached the mining area. I saw no people to hide behind or to use in a diversion. There was mining equipment, but most of it was great towers and machines, like the skeletons of some ancient terrible beings brought to life to work the earth.

Eventually Mr. Hunter came to one of the great mine's entrances. I would have imagined some kind of elevator or shack over a hole in the ground, but instead he reached a hole in the side of a small cliff. A rail for mine carts ran into it.

It was no good following him into the mine. I didn't have Mr. Scant's skill at moving in silence. So I considered my mission complete. I could return to Mr. Scant with the location. Nodding to myself in satisfaction, I turned around. That was when a hand fell heavily onto my shoulder.

XXIV
The Deal

For a moment I feared the worst, but then I saw that it was only Mr. Jackdaw. He had a bit of a swollen lip but seemed to be pretending nothing was wrong.

"This is the place, is it? Good work. You have some talent in sneaking around."

"Erm, thank you?" I said.

"There wasn't much of a fight," said Mr. Jackdaw. "I slipped away while the others kept Hunter's men busy, but I'm sure they've all gotten bored of it by now."

We reconnoitered not in the school but back at the hotel. The Valkyrie and Mr. Scant were unfazed by their fight and wanted immediately to know what we had learned. I told them about the mine entrance, and Mr. Jackdaw confirmed it. We set to strategizing about getting into the mine unseen—and how to deal with much greater numbers, if the Society presence below was formidable.

"What about Mr. Hunter?" I said. "Can you fight him?"

"I don't know," said Mr. Scant. "I think so. He's lost his way."

"Sounds to me like he knows exactly what he's doing," said Mr. Jackdaw. "He's just chosen his secret society over the Crown."

"Maybe he's right, and this will help people," I said.

"Master Oliver, we're not here to deal with politics or save the world," said Mr. Jackdaw. "Your Hunter and his men have their fight and they're the ones who'll fight it. We're not their saviors. The only thing we can do here is focus on our task, which is recovering the diamond."

"But is it really *right*?" I asked.

"Something was stolen and it's our responsibility to recover it. That's all that matters."

"Mr. Scant, do you agree?"

"What we founded the Society to accomplish and the road Hunter's being led down by Aurelian Binns are not the same," he replied. "And if he sells that diamond, I fear he'll see consequences far beyond what he intends."

As the adults continued talking, I went to the window and looked out at the people walking across Kimberley. They didn't appear to need saving, by and large. Some were poor, some were clearly wealthy. Some looked happy, some distressed. I remembered Mr. Sam, who I thought would be so angry and pitiable but who had the most honest smile I had seen since little Victor in France.

"What if we let the exchange take place and then set ambushes?" Mr. Scant was saying.

"I cannot countenance a sale of that diamond to go through," said Mr. Jackdaw. "It's a symbol of the Crown. And I cannot let the deal happen, symbolically."

"Aurelian Binns will be the exchange's middle man, no doubt," Mr. Scant said.

"Isn't that strange?" I said. "Why does he need to be involved? Why doesn't he just let Mr. Hunter make the sale?"

"I imagine young Aurelian has made himself essential to the process," said Mr. Jackdaw.

"I don't like it," I said. "He's always one step ahead of us. Like he knows what we're going to do before we do it."

Mr. Scant reached out to straighten my collar and nodded as if satisfied. "I may have warned you against being arrogant, Master Oliver, but there's no need to be too humble, either. He's no more intelligent than you are."

"He doesn't have to be intelligent," I said. "He just always has a plan. It's like doing magic, I suppose. He knows how to misdirect us. We start thinking we're ahead of him by taking the sceptre away, but he catches us with it. He sends us on a boat to New York, but really he's going to Africa. He tells Mr. Hunter what to say so that we don't know where to be." At that moment, something struck me. "Hold on. Why do we think this exchange happens tomorrow?"

"Because the Binns boy was one day behind Hunter in setting off for Africa," said Mr. Jackdaw. "And . . . because that's what Hunter said to us . . ."

"If we could be here two days faster than Mr. Hunter," I said, "who's to say that Aurelian couldn't have gone that fast too?"

The adults looked at me for a few seconds, and then at once, Mr. Scant and Mr. Jackdaw grabbed their jackets.

"We need to get there," said Mr. Scant. "We need to get there now."

It had been little more than a hunch, but we started to believe in my theory when we saw three of the men from earlier stationed outside the mine entrance through which Mr. Hunter had disappeared.

"They really came," was all the tallest of the men said, while the shortest disappeared into the mine.

"I'll stop that one," Mr. Scant said, already in pursuit of the small man, his golden claw flashing in the bright sunshine.

The third man, the one with the scarred lip, pulled out an iron pipe and ran to intercept Mr. Scant. Mr. Scant deflected the man's first blow, and then Mr. Jackdaw was there to twist the man's wrist and take the pipe from him. Mr. Scant disappeared inside the mine as our fight outside began in earnest. The Valkyrie had drawn her cleavers, but I noticed she was using them backwards, so that when she struck the tall man, it was with the blunt end rather than the blade. This staggered him, and he looked furious.

I gathered dust and threw it in the eyes of the man with the scarred lip so that Mr. Jackdaw could knock him down with the pipe, which made the man go, "Okay, okay, enough, I'm done." This seemed to dishearten the other man, who dropped his own club and shrugged.

"You people are crazy," said the man with the scarred lip. "And it's too late. You can't stop this from happening."

Inside the mine, we didn't know whether to call for Mr. Scant or to keep silent. We found him at a fork in the tracks. From there, the mine cart rails went into two separate shafts. The smallest man lay unconscious, propped up in between the two.

"This way," Mr. Scant whispered.

"How can you be sure?" Mr. Jackdaw asked.

"I can hear them," said Mr. Scant. I strained my ears but heard nothing.

More guards stood along the path, which gave us confidence we were going in the right direction. Some were armed with pistols, but every time, Mr. Scant surprised them, his claw at their necks before they could so much as take aim. Most of them tried to parry Mr. Scant's claw away and attack, but the Valkyrie quickly pinned them down. At these junctures, I would wrest the pistols out of the men's hands and keep them with me. I soon began to feel safe with the three adults around me. But I couldn't help but wonder if we'd finally outwitted Aurelian or if we were making this much progress because he wanted us to.

Finally, we came to a mine cart at the end of the rails, empty but for a pair of shovels. I decided to put all the pistols inside and then took one of the shovels for myself. I felt better with something to defend myself with that wasn't as lethal as a gun. Beyond the mine cart was a large open space—some sort of planning office, deep within the Big Hole of Kimberley. Paper diagrams and cross-sections of the mine hung pinned to boards, and three large desks formed a kind of crescent on the office floor. We stayed huddled in the doorway, because there were a lot of people in the space.

I knew Aurelian at once, with his slim face and high cheekbones. I had no idea how he had braved the heat outside, but he was still wearing a frock coat with travel cape. Mr. Hunter was with him, and Mrs. Hunter sat behind her husband. I thought I recognized the other two fighters from earlier, and alongside them were almost a dozen more. Most of these Society members had dark skin, but two light-skinned men stood amongst them, brandishing weapons and looking menacing.

Opposite them was another group of formidable-looking men, six of them. They looked less like a group of brawlers and more like professional soldiers—out of uniform, perhaps, but on duty. They stood around another man with the darkest skin of any of them, his head bald and his half-moon spectacles giving him the air of an accountant. This, I gathered, was the party buying the diamond. The exchange was underway.

"Mr. Hunter, my friend, I am delighted to finally introduce Mr. de Soto," Aurelian said. "He represents the Laborer's Heritage Association of South Africa, and I can give you every assurance he's sympathetic to your most noble cause."

"It's an honor to be doing business with you," the bespectacled man, Mr. de Soto, said, "and to know our funds will be going toward such righteous endeavors."

As introductions came to a close, Mr. Scant gestured for us to shift to a new position behind a water tank. But as we moved, a cry went up from above. A lookout pointed to us, perched in a spot that we hadn't seen from the entrance. "They're here!" he called out. "They've come!"

The Society's brawlers reacted at once, one man

giving signals to the others as they rushed to surround us. The soldier types didn't move. I heard Aurelian say, "Quickly, before they can interfere."

The first Society man to reach us had a club with nails through it, and he was eager for a fight. He swung it down at Mr. Scant, who grunted as he barely managed to deflect it with his claw. One of the white men, bare-chested but for his suspenders, jumped at the Valkyrie with a knife, laughing and showing sharp teeth. I held up my shovel protectively, beginning to wish I hadn't abandoned the pistols.

"This isn't something we can hurry," I heard Mr. Hunter say.

"Give me the diamond, then," Aurelian said. "Go and make sure they don't interfere."

"I think not," said Mr. Hunter. "Your words, my hand. That's what we agreed."

"I'm of the opinion we kill them and say they fell to their deaths," the bespectacled man said.

"Kill one agent of Scotland Yard and too many more will come," Aurelian said. "We just have to finish this *quickly*."

Through the chaos, I glimpsed Mr. Hunter taking out the diamond. It seemed to be from another world, there in the half-light of the mine.

Mr. Jackdaw had seen it too. From somewhere inside his jacket he produced a metal flask, pulled off the cap and threw it near the feet of the closest men, who jumped back in alarm as it exploded.

Aurelian stood to meet Mr. Jackdaw, drawing out a long dagger from the scabbard at his hip, but Mr. Jackdaw hurled himself at Mr. Hunter instead. Instinctively, Mr. Hunter drew the diamond toward himself, but that was what Mr. Jackdaw had been counting on. He threw a nearby rock, striking Mr. Hunter's hand and making him drop the diamond. But Mr. Jackdaw wasn't finished. He pulled a kerchief out of his pocket. Fake diamonds spilled all around the men, each of them looking just like the Star of Africa.

The little bald man's guards were upon Mr. Jackdaw a moment later. "Restrain him," the man said.

"My apologies, Mr. de Soto," said Aurelian, as Mr. Hunter gathered up all the diamonds. "I did not foresee this."

"No matter," Mr. de Soto said, producing a watchmaker's eyeglass. "I will be able to identify the real one with little difficulty."

The battle was becoming hopeless. I swung my shovel wildly, but the man with the club deflected it to the ground, stomping down so that the metal head snapped off and leaving me with little more than a stick. The man with no shirt seized my arms, holding me so that I could not escape. The Valkyrie and Mr. Scant now had five or six opponents each, which was too much even for them.

As I struggled in the Society man's grasp, I watched in the distance as Mr. Hunter stepped forward and snatched the eyeglass from Mr. de Soto's face.

"What are you doing?" said Aurelian.

Mr. Hunter ignored him, keeping his eyes locked on Mr. de Soto. "Why do you have this?" he asked, pointing to the bald man's eyeglass.

"Wh-what do you mean?" Mr. de Soto replied. "It's an essential tool in our line of—"

"This eyeglass comes from this mine," Mr. Hunter said. "From the Big Hole. Only Union employees from *this* company have these eyeglasses. Men on the payroll of Basil Fields. Why do you have them?"

"I borrowed them," said the old man, who I could just about see from my position was missing some teeth. He licked his lips uncomfortably.

"Who do you work for?"

The little bald man stared at Mr. Hunter for a moment, then croaked, "Seize him."

The guardsmen did as they were told. Mr. Hunter jumped back in alarm and gave a loud whistle. Abruptly, the pressure on my arm stopped. The Society's brawlers—including the man who had held me—were running to help Mr. Hunter, who strained barehanded to defend himself against two batons.

"Damn it all," said Aurelian, and from inside his waistcoat produced a tiny revolver. He cocked the hammer and levelled it, and I was surprised to see he was pointing it at Bartholomew Hunter.

Without thinking, I found myself running forward. I had nothing but the broken shaft of an old shovel—but just maybe I could push Aurelian's hand away.

It was not a lunge that would have earned me a place on the school fencing team, but the pointed tip of the broken shovel found Aurelian's knuckle, bumping the revolver just enough that he fired above Mr. Hunter's head, not through it.

Aurelian bared his teeth at me, but others were coming for him too. The deal was off, and he knew it. "I learned this one from the Claw," he said, and from somewhere on his person he produced a vial shaped to look like an hourglass. He threw it on the ground, where it rapidly began letting off smoke.

"I learned it too," the Valkyrie said, running forward into the smoke. "Got you!" I heard her say—but when the smoke cleared, she was holding only a cloak.

The bald man's six guardsmen were fierce fighters, with no qualms about striking heavy blows to the heads of the men attacking them, knocking them insensible. When one grabbed Mr. Hunter, his wife got up and started trying to pry the guardsman's fingers away, but she was knocked to the ground. Then Mr. Scant appeared, his claws flashing out and cutting the side of the guardsman's wrist.

For a moment, Mr. Scant and Mr. Hunter stood side by side, not sharing glances but aware of one another. I couldn't know for certain, but I was sure they had done this many times before. And then they were rushing forward, coming to the aid of the less well-trained men Mr. Hunter had brought to this underworld deal. Claw and fist pushed the armored men back. Mr. de Soto wanted no more part of this. "Get me out of here," he said to the nearest man. To the others, he snapped, "Kill them all!"

The hired guards were capable fighters. I knew I wouldn't stand a chance against them. Mr. Scant and Mr. Hunter were able to hold their own, but they were outnumbered. When Mr. Hunter tried to break through the line of men to pursue Mr. de Soto, he received a fist to the side of his ribs. Mr. Scant went to support him, but one of the men lashed out with a knife, cutting through Mr. Scant's black jacket and perhaps into his shoulder. Mr. de Soto was out of sight, still yelling orders as he disappeared down a tunnel with his protector keeping Mr. Jackdaw at bay.

Just as I resolved to throw myself into the fight, the Valkyrie made her appearance with a roar. She had found the base of a mine cart and had lifted the whole thing to use as a shield as she charged the five men. Some tried to stab through the wood and one even aimed for the Valkyrie's fingers, but their attacks were nothing before this display of force. The Valkyrie simply flattened them all, then dropped the mine cart base beside her, where it sent up a cloud of dust.

"Fine work!" Mr. Jackdaw said as he ran over. "Oh, you angel!"

"Please stop calling me names like that," said the Valkyrie. "I am not an angel, I am a Valkyrie, and I would have you to watch your tongue."

"Oh. Of course," said Mr. Jackdaw, and set

about helping the society men restrain the guards. Soon they were all subdued, and the mood quickly changed. Men were clapping one another on the back and cheering. They called out challenges and jeers in the direction Mr. de Soto had disappeared. One came to shake each of our hands in turn. This, I had to admit, was a Society quite unlike the one I'd encountered in England.

Mr. Jackdaw, meanwhile, had gathered up all the diamonds, fake and real.

"I want you to give those to me," said Mr. Hunter. I couldn't tell if his words contained a threat or not.

"How will you know which one is real?" I said.

"We'll find a way."

"I think not," said the Valkyrie, as she and Mr. Scant joined Mr. Jackdaw in a defensive posture.

"This is finished, Hunter," said Mr. Scant. "You'll have to kill us to take the diamond back."

Mr. Hunter thought about that for a moment. Then he waved a dismissive hand at us. "I always hated admitting you were right. But it's not worth endangering my men. We fought a good fight today. And there will be other ways for us to fight our battles here. There's no deal. It was all a lie. I don't even know for certain if the real diamond is there at all."

"Wait—what do you mean?" I asked. "What was a lie?"

Mr. Hunter's lip curled in distaste. "The buyer. It was the enemy all along. That man, de Soto, he was from the Union Corporation, Basil Fields's company. Selling the diamond to men like that would have been bad enough. But if I'd given him our story that the one in London is fake, it would have allowed the Union Corporation to discredit the Premier Mine and probably buy them out. The end of the last great independent mine—we'd have been in an even worse situation than before. So I suppose . . . I should thank you."

His wife stepped up to join him. "Why do you need to do that?" she said. "Heck and his friends did nothing. You would have seen the eyeglass anyway and put a stop to the deal."

"Maybe," Mr. Hunter said. "But maybe that poor excuse for a human being de Soto would never have taken out his eyeglass without the fakes. And the boy here stopped a man from shooting me, which I may have deserved for trusting Aurelian Binns. I've seen my folly there. Gray, on the other hand?" He flashed a grin at Mr. Scant. "Well, he caused a brief delay, at least."

"So what now?" I said. "Shouldn't we go after Mr. de Soto? And put a stop to Mr. Fields?"

"We don't need your help fighting our battles. You got what you came for, your stolen diamond. The rest is nothing to do with you. The political system here won't be brought down with a broken shovel. That struggle is for us, and trust me when I say we have heroes of our own. But tonight, you can at least enjoy our hospitality. We had a party planned for after this deal made our dreams come true. Well, the dreams are dashed, but the party is still on. Come along, won't you?"

"I don't like parties," said Mr. Scant. "But very well."

XXV
Fire, Drums, and Steam

T he party was very, very loud.

Ten men played drums around the fire as others danced and ate meat cooked on grills over hot coals, the most incredible smells rising up into the air. Young men I had snatched guns from only hours earlier pulled me up to dance. I didn't know what I was doing, but I hopped from foot to foot and hoped for the best. Mr. Scant, Mr. Hunter, and Mrs. Hunter sat at a table nearby, talking about old times. The Valkyrie had seen Mr. Jackdaw sitting alone and looking abashed, so she went over and invited him to dance. He eagerly accepted, and the two of them began an awkward waltz to the rhythm of the drums.

After Mr. Hunter's associates grew bored with my attempts to dance and left me alone, I went for some meat and took my plate to eat at the edge of the party ground. Not long after I sat down, someone came to sit beside me. In a shirt with an open collar and simple black pants, he looked different, but I still almost choked when I recognized that long hair and thin, serious face.

"Don't be alarmed," Aurelian said. "I thought it would be interesting to talk."

"What do you want?" I said as sharply as I could.

"What do I want? A sale that could have fractured this country away from the Empire—that would have been a start. Between the Union Party finally getting complete control and these Society men getting enough money to fund an uprising, we could have seen a bloody revolution. Can you imagine it? Perhaps it will still happen. Aside from that, well, with my share I could have brought together a society of brothers and sisters such as the world has never seen. One that would embody everything my father wanted but failed to bring to life. I suppose I'm a poor excuse for a Frankenstein, just as he was."

I shifted away from the older boy, ready at any moment for him to strike. "I knew your father and I think you're just like him."

"You mean to be cruel, but that's something I've

always wanted to hear," said Aurelian. He seemed to be watching Mr. Scant, as though wary Mr. Scant would sense him from the other side of the dusty field. "One day I shall have my father back."

"Much good may it do you," I snapped.

"You realize your man over there isn't telling you the whole truth, don't you? About who he is?"

"I realize that, Aurelian, yes. But when has Mr. Scant ever told the whole truth?"

"Perhaps one day I'll get my mother to explain it all to you," Aurelian said. "Well, the woman I call my mother."

"What makes you think I want anything more to do with you?"

"You don't have a choice, Oliver Diplexito." The fire in his eyes made me shudder when I met them. "You're a thief more than I am, because you stole the life I was meant to have. You're the reason we're both here, at the other end of the world."

He raised a hand to my cheek in a callous imitation of affection. "I won't stop until I've taken everything away from you."

I batted his hand away. "I'm not afraid of you. Whatever you try and do, I'll be there to stop it happening."

"I'm counting on it," he said, his cruel expression softening. "You and I are going to shape the world. And the beautiful thing is that you'll have no idea how you're doing it. Enjoy your food. And give my regards to your parents."

"I will do no such thing," I said. He stood and walked away with a mocking bow, and I breathed a sigh of relief.

I didn't mention the encounter to the others when the party ended. What could they have said to help me make sense of it? They would probably have wanted to know why I hadn't called for help or tried to apprehend him or any other pointless thing that would only have made me feel weak. It stung a little—the only reason we had gone to the mine at the right time was that I assumed Aurelian would be one step ahead, and indeed he was.

He occupied my thoughts even as I boarded the train that would eventually take us to a port where we could catch a steamer back home. Back to school and fencing club and probably visits from Mr. Jackdaw and Miss Cai to talk about the international police project that Aurelian so despised. The railway would take us on British land almost the whole way home, land claimed by explorers and bought or perhaps seized from the native peoples.

We made no difference, I thought as I looked out of the window at the dry expanse we were passing. I had gone to Africa imagining we were going to save the day. And we'd recovered the stolen diamond, yes—somewhere among Mr. Jackdaw's fakes, anyway. But I had to wonder what good that did. A diamond in a rod, locked up in the Tower for occasional guests to see, no way of knowing if it was real or a fake. I thought of Mr. Sam and wondered if that was a worthwhile exchange, his arms for pretty stones forever out of reach.

The Empire was vast and unwieldy. To survive, it had to take control. If it showed weakness, another empire would simply take its place. The British would be replaced by the French or the Dutch or the Spanish or the Moors or the Japanese. But what did it mean to be a mighty empire? If the British had not taken diamonds and turned them into armies and guns, would we be the ones who had to form secret societies to stop our votes being taken away? And did that truly make any of it worthwhile?

The Valkyrie came to sit opposite me. "What are you thinking about?"

"Empire," I said. "Is it fair? I understand that you either make an empire or you are made part of an empire. But . . . is it fair?"

"Nothing is," she said.

"I suppose not," I said. Outside our train, the miles of baked earth, shrubs, and skinny little trees were swallowed by the walls of a tunnel, and everything became a rushing black mass.

Mr. Scant had overheard our conversation. "Empire is an expression of arrogance," he said. "It starts in arrogance and can only exist through arrogance. An empire must begin with the idea that it will leave the world a better place than it finds it."

"But the arrogant man falls first," I said. "What about an arrogant empire?"

"It will fall, just the same," said Mr. Scant.

As we emerged from the tunnel, I could see a river far away. "And what about secret societies?"

"There's no more arrogant thing in all the world."

I let out a breath. "Mr. Scant?"

"Yes, Master Oliver?"

"I want to learn everything. Again. Everything we learned together, from the beginning. Will you go on being my teacher?"

Mr. Scant smiled, just a little. "On one condition."

"What's that?"

"Simple. This time, I'll have you teach me too."

"I don't know how much I have to teach. But I'll do my very best."

Mr. Scant nodded. "Let's go home."

About the Author

Bryan Methods grew up in a tiny village south of London called Crowhurst. He studied English at Trinity College, Cambridge, and has recently completed a PhD on First World War poets. He currently lives in Tokyo, Japan, where he loves playing in bands, fencing, and video games.